Giving Ground

Giving Ground

Stories

To Phil

Very best wishes

Colm O'Gaora

Colm O'Gaora

Jonathan Cape
London

First published 1993

1 3 5 7 9 10 8 6 4 2

© Colm O'Gaora 1993

Colm O'Gaora has asserted his right under the Copyright, Designs and Patents
Act, 1988 to be identified as the author of this work

These stories previously appeared in the following publications:
'Magnets' in *Cosmopolitan* and *Best Short Stories* (Heinemann, 1991) and
'Tell Me' in *The Sunday Tribune*.

First published in the United Kingdom in 1993 by
Jonathan Cape
Random House, 20 Vauxhall Bridge Road, London SW1V 2SA

Random House Australia (Pty) Limited
20 Alfred Street, Milsons Point, Sydney,
New South Wales 2061, Australia

Random House New Zealand Limited
18 Poland Road, Glenfield,
Auckland 10, New Zealand

Random House South Africa (Pty) Limited
PO Box 337, Bergvlei, South Africa

Random House UK Limited Reg. No. 954009

A CIP catalogue record for this book
is available from the British Library

ISBN 0-224-03341-7

Typeset in Bembo 11.5/16 by Pure Tech Corporation, Pondicherry, India
Printed in Great Britain by Mackays of Chatham PLC, Chatham, Kent

CONTENTS

For Alison

BETWEEN WORLDS

IN HER HEART Maureen Kelly knew that she loved her husband. As she lay in their bed beside his sleeping form she tried to remember a time when she did not love him. She could not; not because in old age her memory was failing her, but because he had never given her cause to doubt that he loved her, and throughout their fifty-four years together she had reciprocated that love.

She knew too that there was little time left for him in this world. Lately, his sleep had been interrupted more and more often by violent coughing fits, each of which resulted in the appearance of a dark, damp crescent upon the sheets between his legs. His spittle was flecked with bright blood, and each morning the toilet bowl had a pale pink hue, the colour of roses. It was as if he was slowly leaking away. Even as she lay there next to him she could hear death somewhere in his breath; each breath drawn a struggle as if it were his last, each exhalation a death rattle. Some nights she would lie there in the dark listening out for his breathing so that if he were to breathe his last she would hear it. These lonely, solitary, sleepless nights were laced with apprehension, and resignation to the unknown beyond this life.

But not this night. Instead, she watched the moonlight settle on the far wall of their bedroom; light that had found its way through the gaps between the window-shutters above their heads. Years before she would often open the shutters in the middle of the night and sit upon the pillows to watch the stars as they moved through the sky above her. Now her arthritic knees would not allow her to turn and sit upon the pillows to watch the stars. They pinned her flat against the bed. But she would not have her body deny her such a simple pleasure, so, glancing at her husband to ensure that he was sound asleep, she took the brass-rimmed hand-mirror from the bedside table and, reaching up above her head to open one half of the shutters, caught a reflected fragment of the night sky in the mirror held before her face. Here, frozen in the black glass, she could examine the countless, nameless constellations, each with a life more remote and arbitrary than the life she had known for eighty-two years.

The kitchen was dusted with light the following morning. Michael stood at the door looking out at the sky, wiping spittle from his lips, a stick leaning against his hip. His clothes all but fell from his limbs, held there only by the intersections of his body. His brown-green tweed jacket had faded in the sun and rain to the colour of dry leaves. His boots, rendered shapeless by countless inexpert repairs, allowed water in at every step.

'Maureen,' he said without turning his head to where she

sat at the table behind him, 'I'm away down the boreen to fetch back the goat. It has chewed the rope again.'

She did not reply.

He eased himself down the doorstep with the stick and the sun flooded in through the doorway after he had gone.

Presently a lone hen appeared in the doorway and stood there for a few moments like a dead soul contemplating the Rubicon. It strutted inside and searched along the flagstones for stray seeds and breadcrumbs. Maureen listened to its beak tapping off the floor, as if in imitation of the clock that sat on the middle shelf of the dresser.

When she looked out Michael was only halfway across the small field their house stood in. He jerked from side to side as he placed one foot in front of the other, bearing down on his stick from time to time as he paused for breath. In the distance she could see the goat, chewing on the dandelions that grew at the foot of the dry stone walls separating the boreen from the fields on either side. It would take him a half-hour to reach the goat and more than that to drag the animal back to the iron peg at the corner of the house. She felt his pain in her own bones. She stood watching him until he had reached the mouth of the boreen, and then she turned back into the house to set about making him some lunch.

She took a pan of soda bread from the cupboard and laid it upon the table. She began to cut, slice after slice falling over on to its neighbour until a quarter of the pan was gone.

She unwrapped an oblong of butter and placed it upon the table. Two mugs and plates were set out, side by side. She filled the kettle and laid it half-on, half-off the hottest part of the range that dominated the kitchen. It clicked as it began to heat.

The hen flapped up on to the worktop and settled upon the old valve radio that had not worked for years. Maureen went over and patted the hen's sleek head. She turned the tuning button on the radio and watched the ivory-white indicator progress unsteadily across the dial. She decided to plug it in again. There was nothing but a dull buzz which unnerved the hen.

Years before, she used to listen to the radio when Michael was out working the fields. She would tune in to the cookery hour, the gardening programme, and the weather reports from the coastal stations, listening as she moved about the house. What she most looked forward to was the chat show every morning. She would cease her sweeping and scrubbing, boil the kettle for tea, and sit at the table listening to people talking about their own lives; lives which seemed impossibly different from hers. Sometimes, when one of the callers said something bitter or sad about their life, Maureen would walk to the window and look out to where her husband worked the fields around their cottage, reminding herself of how happy she was to have him as her husband, he who had never raised his voice in anger to her or denied her anything. Behind her the plaintive voice of the caller would drone on and on, the presenter struggling and finally succeeding in stemming the flow of bitterness.

Now the radio was dead. Its dial no longer lit up when she switched it on, although sometimes, as now, the hum from the loudspeaker deceived her. When she reached to unplug the radio she looked at the back panel and saw once again the scrapes and dents around the retaining screws in each of its four corners.

She remembered the day that she had used the carving-knife to undo the screws, how the blade had slipped time and time again as she struggled to free the panel. Eventually the panel had given way, exposing the vulnerable valves and circuits inside. It had taken her but a few seconds to shatter the valves and gouge out the transistors with the knife. Replacing the panel had been more difficult but she managed that too, in the end. It had been almost a week before Michael noticed that the radio no longer worked. He did not mourn its passing and since it had become such an integral part of the house he had no mind to remove it.

The hen began to cluck gently when Maureen set down the plug and stroked the bird's neck. Its tiny eyes stared out into the room and its beak opened and closed almost imperceptibly. Eventually it settled down into its ruff of feathers and fell asleep. Maureen stepped away and went into the bedroom.

Every six months Maureen and Michael took the mattress from their bed and stood it in the doorway between the bedroom and the big kitchen so that the flow of air would refreshen its crushed, matted fibres, removing the stale smell of sleep. Afterwards they would return it to the bed, each time alternating which side would face upwards. This ritual had been observed rigidly ever since they had bought the mattress fifty-three years beforehand in a furnishing store in Galway City.

Maureen threw the pillows into the corner of the room then pulled off the sheets which she loosely folded and placed on the floor in front of the wardrobe. The surface of the mattress was more stained than ever before: dark red rings of blood and dead yellow blooms of urine. She could even make out the features of his lower limbs where the fluids had run along the cloth beneath his skin. Upon that mattress there were countless unseen stains, silently chronicling their lives. The blood stains from their wedding night, the spilled semen of decades past and pleasures almost forgotten, their son's afterbirth, and the wasted, discharged fluids of two subsequent miscarriages.

She grabbed the edge of the mattress and pulled hard. After five or six such pulls she had the mattress halfway off the bed, its leading edge just resting on the floor. Ten minutes later the mattress was standing in the doorway between the kitchen and the bedroom.

Maureen waved away the dust and fibres floating in the air around her face and went to the front window which she pushed open. She rested upon the sill and looked out to where she could see Michael's cap appearing over the top of the boreen wall. The cap moved only intermittently and she imagined that he was pausing to rest on his stick, or to look the goat in the eye and curse at it in Irish. She turned her gaze towards the ground in front of the window. The sun had not risen high enough to embrace the front of the house and she could still trace the silvered tracks of snails and slugs across the grass and the heavy, flat clod-breaking stone that had lain there for years now, no longer needed. With a smile she remembered how he used to loop a rope through the hole in the front of the stone and then attach it to the horse's harness. Once at the edge of the unbroken field he would hop up on the stone and urge the horse onwards, dragging both the stone and him behind it, the clods of earth shattering and crumbling as the stone bore into them. Now the only things broken against its worn, pock-marked surface were snail shells when thrushes caught them unawares in the early-morning light.

When she heard him tying the goat to the downpipe at the corner of the house she rinsed and scalded the teapot then dropped three spoons of tea into the bottom and filled it with boiling water. She set the teapot at the edge of the range to draw.

'That Jezebel of a goat will be the death of me yet,' wheezed Michael as he scraped the soles of his boots against the doorstep. 'She has no idea of right or wrong. No consideration for me at all, the bitch. Doesn't she know I've better things to be doing?' His voice was weak, the words forced out with his breath. He paused for breath, staring down at the stone floor, his thumbs looped into the belt of his trousers.

Maureen lifted the teapot from the range and from it filled his mug with dark tea. She placed a knife across a plate, letting the blade rattle against the porcelain, signalling that his food was ready.

He sat down and with his liver-mottled hands took a piece of bread from the carving-board in the middle of the table. Maureen picked his stick from where it rested against his knee and hooked it over the back of his chair. As he ate he looked out through the door at the fields beyond. Cloud shadows progressed slowly across the expanses of potatoes and grass, and in the distance a few rainclouds threatened.

'Rain is forecast,' he said through a mouthful of bread.

Behind him Maureen nodded and looked out along the line of his sight at the rainclouds. She knew that he could tell by the way the wind was blowing that the rain would not fall upon their roof today, otherwise he would have told her to take the clothes in off the bushes where she had earlier stretched them out to dry. Nevertheless, he had forecast rain and it would undoubtedly fall, elsewhere.

She pulled out a chair and sat opposite him before filling her own mug with tea. She poured milk first into his tea and then into her own. Although she was exhausted and her arms ached from lifting and moving the mattress she had no appetite. The effort still clung in her throat and she declined to take some bread from the carving-board when he nudged it towards her. While she slowly sipped tea from her mug he ate in silence, his jaws making exaggerated movements as he chewed the dry soda bread, his eyes fixed on the fields and the sky outside.

The hen fluttered down from its resting-place on top of the radio and went to stand beneath Michael's chair. Its head poked out between his knees as it sought to catch falling crumbs even before they hit the ground. Michael did not seem to notice its presence.

As they sat there across the table from each other with the hen moving about beneath them, Maureen acknowledged again the pitch of their existence. It was the pitch of the note that had been struck on the day after their wedding when she had come to this house to live with him. And still it reverberated soundlessly in the air around them. She felt it along the fire-iron when she thrashed the dust from the floor-mats; she felt it when she beat the hearth with a block of timber to loosen the soot that had built up inside; and she had felt it in the quivering form of the mattress during each of the one-hundred-and-eight times that they had hauled it upright in the bedroom doorway.

Quite suddenly, Michael dropped his mug of tea on the table. It did not spill but the heavy crockery base made a loud retort against the hard wooden surface. The hen let out a squawk and ran from beneath the table and out through the door. Maureen looked at her husband's face and followed his stare to the doorway between the kitchen and the bedroom where the mattress now stood, benefiting from the draught that ran between the two rooms. Michael swallowed his mouthful of bread.

'The mattress is up, Maureen,' he said, his voice coarse, as if strained through rough sackcloth. 'The mattress is up.'

Maureen looked at him and raised her eyebrows, her lips pursed tightly in defiance of what she knew he must say.

'It is fifty-four years since either of us turned that mattress of our own accord, Maureen, and I wished to be in the grave before either of us would need to turn it on their own again.' He leaned forward on his elbows and coughed for a few seconds, blood returning momentarily to his cheeks with the strain.

He coughed again and she pushed the mug of tea into his outstretched fingers, bidding him to drink from it. As she did so he grabbed for her hand and wrapped his fingers tight around it. In astonishment she lifted her face up and caught the depths of his eyes, cataract-scarred, one gone cloudy with glaucoma, the myriad thin lines upon the skin around them like the threads that joined and intersected their lives.

'Are you burying my body before my soul has given it up to the Lord?' he said.

No, she mouthed back, her eyes fixed upon his which were softening now.

'I don't doubt you, Maureen, but there are things we have always done together, things that we will always do together.'

Reaching behind him for his stick he pushed back the

chair and stood up slowly. He went out, the point of his stick thumping off the ground as he walked.

In his wake Maureen stared at his plate with its half-eaten slice of bread, a knob of soft butter melting on top. The knife lay between the plate and the half-empty mug, and crumbs and drops of tea speckled the table where he had sat. She continued staring at them for a minute or so.

She had no words to answer him, only her expressions. Her stare turned towards the three piles of notebooks, warped with damp and mildew, that lay on top of the dresser in the darkest corner of the kitchen. The first of them had lain there for eleven years, the last of them for maybe eight. She could not remember what was in those notebooks but knew that if she were to take one down and flick through its pages it would be her neat handwriting that she would find there, her questions and replies, her needs and desires. An impression of herself from those first few years after the operation that had saved her life but removed her larynx.

The hen reappeared in the doorway but Maureen had no time for it now. She got up and shooed it out of the kitchen then followed it outside.

The rainclouds had disappeared from the horizon to be replaced by a defiantly blue sky. The sound of a cuckoo rang in the air and Maureen searched the tops of the stone walls for the bird, but it was nowhere to be found. The goat rubbed its flank against the wall of their cottage, the whitewash coming off on its coat. She felt sorry for the poor animal, tethered now by the shortest of ropes, too short for it to reach with its mouth.

In the vegetable plot at the side of the house Michael was hoeing weeds from between the cabbage drills. He leaned upon his stick with one hand and swung the blade of the hoe loosely up and down with the other. It missed its target more often than not, cutting through the tender leaves of the young cabbages, and even once splitting the soft crown of one of the plants. Maureen could see him muttering curses to himself, spittle flying from his lower lip. A breeze picked up and caught a cloud of dust in its grip carrying it up into the old man's face. He shut his eyes tightly and continued with his hoeing, the action no more inaccurate now than when he could see.

She watched him, knowing that inside himself he was working away the seed of anger that had begun to germinate when he had seen the mattress. It had been an intimation of mortality, and he refused to acknowledge that his time was drawing nearer, refused to believe that he would depart this world, these fields, this earth.

He was a man of the earth, of stone and clay, and for her he *was* the earth. Once, he had farmed all these fields around their cottage, turned the soil with his own hands, broken it with the breaking-stone, and cut the hay from dawn to dusk each August. Now that land lay in the hands of younger, more ambitious men, who farmed with tractors and hired labour for the harvest season.

Michael had provided everything for her in the fifty-four

years of their marriage and it had been he who produced the first notebook in the hospital a week after her operation. She had smiled to herself and pretended not to notice when she opened it and found the blurred ink-stamp on the inside cover – the stamp of the school their son taught in. It had not been Michael's idea after all, but for three years she had filled page after page with silent speech. Eventually an unwritten, wordless language had evolved between them and there was no longer any need to write things down.

She had never questioned her fate, had never racked against the reality that she would not speak another word as long as she lived. It was God's will, and His alone. His will was inseparable from her life, as it was inseparable from the ending of her husband's life.

She watched him working for a while longer. Every so often he would rest the handle of the hoe against the hollow of his stomach, touch the rim of his cap and look up. He would not look in her direction for it was not from there that the weather came, but from the south-west. She put her hands deep down inside the pockets of her apron and breathed in deeply. The honeysuckle that grew at the back of the house was in bloom and its scent filled her.

It was on days such as this that she missed the sound of the radio most. Fine, dry days when Michael spent every hour in the fields, tending to what few animals were left, watering and weeding the vegetable plot. These were the days, like those interminable hospital days, when she felt most alone with herself. Yet she knew that it was she who had resigned herself to this aloneness, this silence.

While she leaned back against the thick door-frame she remembered each and every step she had taken from her hospital bed to the public telephone at the end of the ward. With each careful step she continued to listen to the chat show on the transistor radio beside her bed, mouthing the telephone number of the radio station to herself, setting out in her own mind what she would say to the presenter when her turn came to talk.

Her turn never came. When the radio station's telephonist answered, Maureen was transfixed, frozen by a truth just revealed to her. Thick gurgles and hisses emanated from her throat when she went to speak. Pain fizzed behind her tongue and she put a hand to her throat. The telephonist said *hello* two or three times before the line clicked dead. Maureen held the handset to her ear and stared out of the window at four men playing golf on the course beyond the hospital grounds. She could almost hear the sound of their laughter, cajoling each other as they prepared to swing, whistling as a golf ball sped through the air. Behind her, voices babbled from the transistor radio. And as she listened and stared her throat continued to gurgle and hiss. Tears began stepping down her morphine-swollen, paper-white cheeks. Some collected in the mouthpiece. For the first time, anger rose slowly inside her and she squeezed her eyes shut, wincing with the pain, lifting her heels clear of the ground in frustration. A nurse found her minutes later, the telephone draped over her arm, her forehead resting against the window, tears cutting through the film of dust upon the glass.

Eleven years later, that pain was still felt. Michael saw it as he turned away from the row of cabbages and looked at her standing in the doorway of the cottage. Even at this range he knew what she was thinking about, and when she looked up and caught his face turned upon hers she knew that he knew. He waved but she did not see his hand against the brightness of the sky behind him.

The good weather of that May continued for the rest of summer. Michael spent his last months looking after the vegetable plot and every now and again retrieving the goat from the end of the boreen. At the end of July he gave the goat to one of the neighbouring farmers to sell at the market in Maam Cross. The few pounds it raised paid for a new coat of whitewash on the outside walls of the cottage. With the goat gone from the side of the house, daisies, clover and cowslip began appearing through the grass, turning the field in which the cottage stood into a mass of pale purples, whites and yellows. The fuchsia bush at the gate burst into flower and the sweet-pea that Maureen had planted at the gable-end added to the riot of colour.

Michael took to remarking upon the emergence of each individual blossom, and Maureen noted that as the days slowed for him every tiny detail of life made a difference.

He did not speak of death, only of life. During those few months the death of Maureen's second cousin was not recorded within the four walls of the cottage, yet the news of the birth of a distant grand-niece in August was received by Michael with almost unbridled joy and, Maureen suspected, a kind of relief.

Towards the end Michael spent more and more time inside the house. He lay on the bed in the afternoons, not sleeping but staring up at the ceiling, his breath wheezing in the late-summer heat. When he wasn't lying on the bed he was sitting in front of the window watching the farmers cutting the hay in the adjoining fields. He only ventured out to collect the bouquet of fragile flowers for the vase upon the dresser. Maureen felt that her own private space had been invaded. The house was her domain, the fields his, but she would not deny him comfort in his last days.

On the night before he died Maureen lay in bed, her arms crossed above the blankets, her eyes wide open in contemplation of the light playing upon the far wall of the bedroom. Every so often she glanced at the door into the kitchen behind which Michael still sat, sipping the warm milk she had heated for him a half-hour before. As she listened to him coughing she wondered how much time he had left in this world, before he passed into the next. She reached up and pushed open one of the window-shutters. Moonlight flooded the room, rendering every-thing the colour of dark cadmium. Taking the hand-mirror from the bedside cabinet, Maureen held it out in front of her and manoeuvred it so that it held the stars inside its frame.

These distant, dying suns seemed more incandescent than ever before, as if they were all about to die at once and were expelling every element of energy in one final glorious burst.

She peered at the constellations, mapping them out in her memory, noting how their configuration had changed as the earth swung around the sun. And as she watched the stars the efforts of the day began to take their toll so that eventually sleep overtook her.

When she woke the room was still in darkness. Her fingers brushed the cool surface of the hand-mirror where it lay across her stomach. She reached over to where Michael slept but his side of the bed was empty. Then she remembered and looked over at the door into the kitchen. Suddenly she was afraid.

She opened the door and stood in the doorway for a few seconds, listening. There was nothing but the throb of the night inside her ears, the beating of her heart, and the breath catching in her throat. The kitchen was engulfed in an impenetrable darkness. Putting her hands out in front of her she inched her way across the floor towards where she knew the oil lamp would be. Her hands found nothing but an empty, polished surface where

the lamp should have been. She could feel the specks of
wax that had, over the years, dripped from the tapers they
used to light the wick. Her breathing quickened as some
unknown fear developed within her. It drummed inside
her ears as she turned around to face the expanse of the
black room.

Michael's face was so pale as to be quite visible in the
profound blackness of the kitchen. He was standing upright
in front of the range, his arms hanging at his sides, his eyes
trained upon the shape of his wife as she moved towards
him through the inked air.

As she came to stand in front of him she saw the wetness
in his eyes, how his whole body shook with fear. She knew
that at last he had embraced the truth of his existence.

'I am between this world and another now,' he said,
reading her thoughts. His voice was soft and clear, but
resigned. A voice she had not heard before.

She reached for his wrist and to her surprise was able to
encircle it with her thumb and forefinger. How thin he
was! Nothing but dry bone and ligament. She lifted his
hand and placed it at her throat. His fingers pressed against
the scar upon her neck.

'If you could talk again, Maureen, what would you say
to me now?'

His words hurt her in a way nothing he had said over the
last eleven years had hurt. Here, in the darkness at the end
of his existence where he could barely read her face, his
words cut through the air and her inability to talk saddened

her. She could not reply, only nod in acknowledgement, not knowing whether he could see her or not.

His fingers were cool against her skin as they traced the curving line of the shallow scar. She felt goosepimples hooping around her neck. Raising her hands she touched his cheek and it too felt cold to touch. She wanted to fall against him then, to tell him that she loved him and would not let him slip away from her; but that privilege had been denied her for years and it was no different now.

Michael began to mumble to himself in Irish. The dense words filling the air around them had the thick rhythm of prayers or old proverbs. His lips rattled together forming sequences of syllables as he breathed in and out. She knew now how desperate he was to make his peace with the world before he left it. She thought of going out to get the priest to hear Michael's last confession, but dismissed it in case he would die before she returned.

His fingers slid away from the scar and into her thin, fine hair. The prayers ceased and he pulled her head to his shoulder. She leaned into him, feeling the angle of his collar bone pressing against her forehead. His arms tightened across her back as he pulled her closer and closer and she felt the trembling that had taken over his whole body. She felt too that he was tired in a way he had never been before; that the wonders and agonies of life had washed through him, leaving behind this dry, brittle frame, and exhausted mind.

With her fingers she found his mouth. His lips were dry

and cracked, the legacy of countless seasons. She felt his tongue pressing against the inner edge of his lips and she realised that it could come no further, that his mouth was dry too. She moistened her own lips and guided them to his. As they kissed she opened her eyes and looked up at him. His eyes, the eyes she had known for a half-century, were open at that moment, taking in the shadowed landscape of her face, reconstructing her features in the darkness.

'You . . . have loved me . . . enough, Maureen,' he said when she drew her lips away.

She kissed him again, this unfamiliar but unforgotten simple act speaking for her, telling him that she would always love him.

He died, as he had lived, in the fields. Maureen found him early the next morning, crouching amidst the clover and cowslip at the side of the cottage. As she walked towards him in the fragile light of dawn she saw the silver sheen of dew upon his jacket and along the nape of his neck and she knew that he was dead. She continued to walk, noticing the sun rising above the distant steeple of their parish church.

He had fallen forward as he died and his hands were stretched out in front of him. A grey slug made its way across the back of his left hand. Wound between his fingers were the broken fragments of a daisy-chain, the petals withered and bruised now, the stems blackened where he had pierced them with his fingernail. Maureen bent down and flicked the slug from his cold skin. She picked up the daisy-chain and pushed it carefully into the pocket of her apron. Then, not looking back, she set out to walk the two miles to the village.

TELL ME

Somehow, despite his denials, I knew that my father and I had been this way before. A picture of the stone-walled, tree-lined road had hung in my memory and had been carried forward like original sin from that one day in my childhood when I had been driven this same way by him. In those days I had believed, as all children inevitably do, that my father could do no wrong.

I was on my way back to London and he had offered to drive me to the airport. We set off ridiculously early because he had suggested that we drive up into the surrounding hills so that I could look down upon the city that I was once again leaving behind me. He has always been a true romantic, my father, and so I feigned enthusiasm in order to please him. It was indeed a vibrantly sunny day and the warm air throbbed with the expectancy of high summer, lending considerable weight to his argument.

The car brought us swiftly along beneath yawning canopies of leaves which swayed in the breeze, parting just often enough for us to catch glimpses of the city bustling upon the horizon. The heat made my jeans stick to the vinyl car seat and I fidgeted around trying to free myself. Dad didn't seem to notice my discomfort and I put this down to him concentrating on the winding road. I wound the window the whole way down and let the rush of air whip beads of sweat from my forehead, being careful to dodge the flailing roadside briars. Now I was glad that he had brought me up here before I left.

Soon we turned into a road where the stone walls were higher and where the roadside trees entwined overhead, obscuring much of the sunlight. As we swept on into the darkness I turned to look back at the receding city but what glimpses I had had before were blocked now by the closely grown trees. Turning to my father I saw his expression change from one of amused abandon to a bewildered expression that spread across his features and seemed to seep into the air around us.

The childhood memory returned.

'We've been this way before, haven't we, Dad,' I said, turning to look at him.

'No. Well, I don't think so,' he replied. 'It's very different from the rest of the hills around here, isn't it?' He lifted a hand from the steering wheel and gestured towards the dark green canopy above our heads. 'It must be all these trees that do it.'

We continued along the winding road for another two hundred yards or so, Dad almost letting the car roll the distance. We turned left into another road which, although similar, was no more than half the width of the previous one. Blackberry shrubs pushed against the car doors. The road surface was broken by tufts of grass and the tyres crushed the remains of egg shells that had fallen from the branches overhead.

'Are you sure we aren't lost?' I asked as we crept around another bend. 'It looks as if no-one has been here for ages.'

'Don't worry, son, I know where I'm going. I know.'

His head turned slowly from side to side as if looking for an exit at the side of the road, although the obvious path seemed to be to follow the road on down the hill or to reverse all the way back towards the last road we had left behind.

'Ah! I knew it was along here somewhere,' he said, slipping the car into reverse and turning to look between the head-rests as we inched back along the way we had come. 'Who said I was lost?'

I looked over his shoulder and noticed a rusting water pump lurking moss-ridden in the tangle of briars and weeds at the roadside. As he reversed his forearm rested upon my shoulder for a moment. He trembled almost imperceptibly.

He brought the car to a halt. I peered across him to see just what we had stopped at. It was an iron gate, overrun with bindweed that rendered it all but invisible to the uninitiated.

'You *must* have been here before,' I said while I undid my seat-belt. 'How could you have found this unless you knew where to look for it?'

He didn't appear to have heard me and was already getting out of the car. He stepped over to the gate and I noticed that it was well-built and not at all typical of the grid-iron gate so common in any countryside. Tearing the bindweed away from the latch he lifted it and pushed it open. It swung inwards with the shrillest of squeaks and he turned to face me, a look of anticipation upon his face. I peered out at him from inside the car. 'Where's this?' I asked.

'Come on. Don't look so worried,' he said. 'Here, you can drive the car in or have you forgotten *all* I taught you?'

He turned and walked back in between the gateposts while I followed him tentatively in the car. He pushed the gate shut behind me. I parked the car next to a wild and bushy privet hedge, and as I stepped out I noticed that although the ground was now covered in grass it had once been a gravel driveway.

'Come on! We don't have much time to hang around,' he said, disappearing through a gap in the hedge cleverly disguised by its wild branches.

Once on the other side of the hedge I stood quite still. Before me was a bedraggled two-storey house overgrown with clematis and honeysuckle. The humming air was laden with their scent and bumble bees hovered around the building, visiting the plethora of blossoms that exploded across the walls and windows. Paint peeled from the front door in long strips, but the glass in the windows seemed intact, and despite the enveloping greenery the house appeared to be in good condition.

Around the house the garden was a teeming mass of trailing flowers and attendant insects, the grass knee-deep and curved like an angler's rod with the burden of ripening seeds. Dad sneezed violently. The air, thick with pollen, had worked its way into his sinus membranes. He put the back of his hand to his nose and sniffled.

'Yes, son,' he began, 'you were here once before. You must have been no more than three or four years old. I was younger too and this garden was neat and tidy, and that door a bright marine blue. I know because I painted it for her.'

As he spoke, he looked the house up and down with his arms folded, rocking back and forth off the ball of his foot. In his fist he held a large key attached to a leather key-fob I had not seen before.

Opening the door, he allowed me inside first. Sunlight streamed into the room through two bay windows at the rear, although the matrix of branches that criss-crossed the glass cast the complex shadows of a stained glass window. Dust danced in the brilliant shafts of light, the tiny particles assuming their own inner harmony, seeming to exist within individual planes of movement, never colliding with one another. I was mesmerised.

To my right a stairway led upwards to a landing. At the foot of the stairs was an open doorway into a tiled kitchen. A solitary bowl sat in the centre of the table at which two bare, solid chairs stood in expectant silence. A butterfly flitted through the beams of light that filtered into the kitchen, alighting first on the table's edge and eventually coming to rest upon the lone light bulb suspended from the ceiling. In the alcove beneath the stairs a rocking-chair upholstered in deepest burgundy sat awaiting new momentum. I wondered just how long it had waited.

I would have expected an abandoned place like this to smell stale and damp, but instead the air was tinged with the scent of honeysuckle from the plants outside. This lent a further sense of unreality to the house, almost as if time had stood still here since the last occupant had left.

Dad stood at the bay window towards the back of the house. The sunlight streamed in upon him creating a halo effect amongst the thinning hairs on his head. I joined him there; he like a lizard soaking up the rays and the memories, and I like the devious school-child filled with wonder at having fallen upon this secret place. Only this was not simply a secret place to be, it was also a secret place in the depths of my father's memory and I was beginning to feel like an unwelcome intruder, even though it was he that had brought me here.

I could not tell if he had read my feelings from my face but he laid a heavy hand on my shoulder as he turned slowly back into the room. There was no need for him to say anything now, and I had no desire to ask.

As he retreated across the room I wondered how many times he had stood here at the window in the evenings after work with her in his arms, his hands across her tummy, her shoulders resting against his chest. Had he read to her from Keats and Shelley as I remember him doing for my mother, or had they simply stood here enjoying each other's silent company? Had they laughed at each other's idiosyncrasies or at the paleness of their fair skins while they undressed each other in the thickening dusk? I needed no answers now. All was etched into the very character of the house and into the expressions drifting like clouds across his face.

Leaning forward, I carefully unlatched and pushed open one of the windows in front of me. Fragile blisters of crackling paint scattered to the ground. Warm air surged quietly in against my face. I shut the window too suddenly, raising dust from the sill. Outside, a violent gust of wind rushed across the bowing tree tops, startling the insects in its haste.

'Dad,' I called, 'don't forget the time.'

There was no answer, just the creaking of the floorboards above in response to his weight. I went up to join him.

Upstairs was a warren of small rooms, each leading off a central landing. The doors swung easily inwards, thick layers of dust floating from their oak panels and on to the floor as I entered each room in turn. In what must have been the study a sheaf of papers lay on the corner of a writing desk. As I approached I recognised his familiar script in the blue fountain pen he has always preferred. Letter after letter after letter had been begun, and not one completed, the few sentences struck through with a bold yet unsteady line, as if the very act of writing the words again and again had been, and served, his purpose. 'My dearest Caroline,' they each began then drained away, like passion spent. My mother's name. I ran from the room, sending dust spinning in my wake.

At the bedroom I hesitated. Dad stood by the dresser running his finger along the top edge of the mirror and allowing the dust to drift away in small clumps and come to rest on the lace cloth that marked the space where her make-up and powder-puff would have lain. The bedroom was bright and airy, although spiders had colonised a corner of it at one time. Their destitute webs hung drape-like from the coving and swayed in response to our movements.

The large bed was still made, the sheets turned and folded perfectly. A deep red over-blanket had been bleached to a sickly yellow on one side by the sun and as he patted it dust rose in plumes from its surface. I knew that he must have lain many times upon this bed fixing his gaze upon the ceiling or maybe upon her damp down-covered skin after they had made love together one more time before he returned home to his wife and my mother.

As I watched him standing over the bed he appeared to me to be like a mourner crouched in intense and absolute concentration over an ebbing corpse; as if willing life into what lay before him, memories waxing and waning.

She was still there; in his conscience at least, if not elsewhere.

'Dad,' I whispered. 'Let's go – there's no more time.'

'No more time,' he repeated, his voice almost cracking. 'Never was a truer word said.'

At the foot of the stairs he stopped and I brushed past

him. When I reached the door I turned to see where he was. He stood half-hidden in the shadow of the open door of a tall closet. His hand gripped the handle so hard that the blood ran away from his knuckles which now shone white in the gloom. As he drew away from the darkness I saw the dress draped across his forearm, a riot of colour in the pall of shadows at the foot of the stairs. Its collar was vibrant peach and an explosion of blossoms ran from it down to the hem. Few would find it particularly attractive.

He ran a finger along its smooth yielding length, little ripples bounding in front of his finger as it travelled the cloth, ending in a flick and swish of material at the bottom. The dress swung silently like a pendulum weighing time before coming to a halt.

'It was always her favourite dress,' he said, his voice a coarse whisper catching in his throat. He stepped out towards the centre of the room.

From his pocket he drew the brass cigarette lighter my mother had bought for his birthday two years ago. Carefully he unscrewed the reservoir cap and allowed drops of clear lighter fuel to gather and swell before dripping onto the colourful fabric in his other hand. The drips became a trickle shortly before he tightened the cap and stifled the flow. Hanging the dress at arm's length he lit the hem. Blue flames broke in a smile across the blossoms. While he went to drape the burning dress over the rocking-chair I opened the door.

He didn't look back until we had turned the corner on

to the wider road. A plume of smoke rose from a gap amongst the trees before being whisked up and dispersed by a breeze that blew across the side of the hill. Amidst the smoke, black leaves of ash flew about like escaping ghosts. I wound down the window and could barely hear the crackling of flames. The sound of departing insects grew to a cacophony in my ears.

I turned back to face my father, and caught the trailing edge of that last cloud drifting across his face. His eyes were once again on the road.

'Tell me,' I said.

And he did.

FINDING THE SEA

THE RISEN SUN had erased all shadow from the land around the house so that now it stood quite alone amidst its complement of crooked fields. A pillar of brown smoke rose at an awkward slant from the chimney, and a dog still slept in the shelter of the turf stacked against the gable end.

When the boy went to the window he noticed a patch of ragged bog cotton that had broken through the stretch of gravel at the side of the house. He watched it steadily, aware that at any moment the single tuft of white cotton could be torn from its stalk by the wind. And even as he watched, his face pressed against the glass, he imagined that same tuft of teased cotton caught in a breeze, tumbling through the empty air towards an unknown destination. He could not take his eyes from it.

In the next room the voices started up again.

'Don't you think you owe me that much after all this time!'

The previous night, like many nights, had been punctuated by his parents' shouts. Mostly it was his mother's voice that he could hear, but occasionally his father's deeper voice sounded through the door.

'I just wanted one,' he was saying, 'one little drink, that was all . . .' His voice trailed off as she cut him short.

'One little drink is all it takes!' Her hand thumped the table. 'You know that as well as I do.' She made loud clicks in the back of her mouth with her tongue. She did this only when she was very angry. 'Now, look where one drink has got you.' Click. Click. Click. 'You were plastered when you came in last night, Joseph Kavanagh, plastered!'

Cathal remained at the window, his eyes upon the bog cotton, still waiting to watch it disappear. The wind began to gust.

His father went to speak but, instead of talking, he took to mumbling incoherently.

'I am going to get Cathal off to school now.' Click. Click. 'Don't you dare show your face out there until you're sober. Hear?'

The door-handle rattled and Cathal turned away from the window, fixing his eyes upon the school jotter spread out upon the kitchen table. His mother came into the room, breathing quickly through clenched teeth. He smiled at her before turning quickly towards the window.

The white cotton was gone, leaving only a bare stalk, brown and desolate against the hard gravel.

He felt his mother's hand warm upon the crown of his head, her breath heavy against his scalp. She leaned over his shoulder.

'What's out there to be looking at this time of the morning?'

'Nothing, Mam.'

'Just dreaming then, hmm?'

The truth embarrassed him. He looked away from her, at the bags of Odlum's flour and Barry's tea stacked upon the shelves, at the half-empty bottle of stout in the dark corner between the bread-bin and the door. He shrugged his shoulders and she muttered something in Irish that he didn't quite catch.

He felt a trembling start in her hand just as she lifted it from his head. As she turned towards the sink he glanced back at the drawing-room door. It had not closed properly behind her. Between the gap he could see his father standing in the middle of the darkened room, his fingers cupped around his unshaven chin. Although he stood quite still it was easy to tell by the effort of concentration and the weakness in his neck that made his head nod back and forth that he was still quite drunk. Cathal watched as he stepped over to the oak dresser, shiny with the wax polish of many years, and looked at the rows and rows of framed photographs ranged along its shelves. There were pictures there of aunts, uncles, grandparents and cousins who had long since emigrated to America. There was a picture of a hurling team and, beside it, a colour print portrait of the American president, Jeff Kay, as Cathal understood it. His father picked the largest photograph of all from the middle shelf and held it up close. It was a photograph of their wedding day, a close-up of them standing in the wind outside the church in Tuam. His mother's face crowded most of the print, her veil out of focus in front of her face. Visible at her side, but obscured somewhat by the veil and stray locks of her hair, was Cathal's father. The tips of his fingers plucked at his bow-tie and he was looking not at the camera but at his wife, a satisfied smile upon his lips.

Cathal watched, mesmerised, as his father placed the photograph face-down on the counter of the dresser and brought his clenched first sharply down on the back of the frame. The glass shattered and the wooden frame broke with a soft, dull cracking noise.

Cathal turned towards his mother who was working at the sink. She had heard nothing.

When he looked again his father had stood back from the dresser, his fingers splayed out across his eyes and forehead, buried in thought, or remorse. Suddenly, he seemed to feel Cathal's stare and looked around. Their eyes met: Cathal's bright and blue, his father's dark and bloodshot. His father put a finger across his pursed lips. Cathal nodded in return. Between them there was now a conspiracy. He felt it move between them, joining their individual silences.

His attention was drawn away by water gushing from the tap at the sink. Cathal watched as his mother lifted the steaming kettle from the range and added its contents to the laundry in the sink. Plunging her hands in amongst the clothes she began to rub and squeeze, her head craned upwards as if she were trying to look up through the sky and into outer space itself. It was only then that Cathal noticed the tears trickling away from the outer corners of her eyes and trailing across her temples. He watched her in silence, waiting for a sob which never came. Instead she bit on her lip and squeezed her eyes tightly shut, lifting a great lump of sodden, steaming linen from the sink and wringing it tightly in her fists.

The sun had made one edge of Cathal's jotter curl over on itself. He closed the cover and pressed down upon it for a moment before inspecting the straightened page and placing it into his school-bag. He stuck his head through the gap in the drawing-room door to say goodbye to his father. The sound of heavy snoring came to him; his father was slouched in an armchair, his arms dangling over the side.

Cathal went over to the dresser. Pieces of glass had fallen to the floor and the print itself hung over the edge of the counter. It had been made to look like an accident. He looked back at his father, then carefully picked the print from where it lay amongst the shattered glass and frame. He shoved it into his school-bag, flat between his atlas and jotter.

He stepped quietly across the kitchen floor. He wanted to run to his mother and hug her and say goodbye but feeling awkward he crept out the door instead.

She heard his feet crunch on the gravel path outside.

'Bye, son' she called after him, 'pay attention in your maths class today.'

He did not hear her. He was already running off towards the road, his school-bag swinging at his side.

Around him the bogs stretched out to the rim of the

horizon. Cut into the land at irregular intervals were dark rectangles where the first turf of the season had already been saved. The exposed banks of wet peat gleamed in the sun. The turf that had been saved was stacked in pyramids of three or four pieces, spread out to dry amongst the sharp grass and bog cotton. In the distance Cathal could see Feherty's donkey, standing alone in the lee of a rock, a pair of wicker baskets slung over its back. Feherty himself could not be seen, hidden as he was in the depth of a cutting. Cathal's father had often said that Feherty was so mean that he would cut turf so deep that he hit bedrock, and that even then he wouldn't stop cutting.

Ahead of him was the cottage where his friend, Hugh O'Meara, lived. Usually, Hugh waited for Cathal at the rusting gate to his father's cattle field, but today he had decided to leave early. Hugh's father waved at Cathal from the paddock at the rear of the house where he was repairing a broken fence, a dark blur against the sky. He pointed in the general direction of the school-house and shouted something that Cathal didn't quite catch. Then he lifted a mallet and continued driving a stake into the soft ground. As Cathal ran after his friend the sound of each mallet-strike followed him.

'Hugh!' he called, panting as he ran up the gentle incline, 'Hugh, wait will you?' A breeze pulled the words from his mouth. He heard them himself, trailing in his wake. Hugh would never hear them. He ran faster.

Eventually Hugh turned around to look back down the

road and saw Cathal running to catch up with him. Cathal
slowed when he saw Hugh stop and wave. He was dizzy
from running and when he stopped for breath he thought
that he could still hear the sound of feet moving across
gravel; the sound of his father's feet, stumbling down the
path to their cottage last night, then the slump of his
shoulder against the front door, calling out for his wife.

'What kept you this morning?' Hugh asked when Cathal
reached him, hands gripping his knees, staring at the gravel,
catching his breath.

'I . . . I had more homework to do.'

'What? You didn't do it last night.'

'No.' He felt the blood rushing beneath his cheeks, could
feel his lungs filling and ebbing against his rib-cage.

'That's not like you, Cathal Kavanagh, the class genius.'

Cathal straightened himself and looked at his friend. His
black hair was uncombed and there were traces of dried
milk and breadcrumbs on his chin.

'Dad was drinking last night, at home. He started singing
when Mam went out to her meeting in the town. He put
me off.'

'Can't he sing?'

'No, he can't. He thinks he can, but it's just shouts.'

Cathal picked his school-bag off the ground and began
to walk along the road. He did not feel like answering
questions from Hugh about his father. Although they were
best friends he knew that Hugh would let the whole class
know that his father couldn't hold his drink.

They walked towards the school in silence. On either side of them the fields stretched into the distance. Sheep grazed in a few of them, but mostly the land was set out for turf-cutting.

Just as they came in sight of the school-house Hugh stopped dead in his tracks. Cathal had walked on a bit before he noticed.

'I didn't do any homework at all,' said Hugh, not looking up.

'None?'

'None. I just didn't want to do any of it.'

'What'll you do now? Maistir O'Riain will *kill* you, Hugh. You'll get the strap for sure.'

There was a hint of defiance amidst the tears in Hugh's eyes when he looked at Cathal. 'I'm not going to go to school today, Cathal, I'm going somewhere else.' He kicked at a large stone and sent it flying into the shallow ditch between the road and a dry-stone wall.

'But you have to go to school, Hugh, you *have* to,' Cathal protested. 'And where are you going to go anyway?'

'To the sea.'

The words rang in Cathal's ears. He turned to look at the school-house. A group of the younger children stood patiently near the front door, waiting for Miss Toomey to open up at nine o'clock. Two older boys teased a donkey standing in the shadows at one end of the school yard. Beyond the school-house was the church. He watched the cloud of dust thrown up by Mr Cloherty, the sacristan, as he raked the weeds from the path to the church door. It was more or less like this every morning.

Cathal had never been to the sea, had never even seen it for himself. All he knew of it was what he had heard at school and the postcards that arrived from relatives holidaying in Salthill or Rosses Point.

'The sea?' he enquired quietly, breathlessly. 'Where?'

'Anywhere! I don't know.' Hugh glanced nervously at the group of children outside the school-house. 'Make your mind up quick before we're seen. Are you with me or not?'

Cathal looked again at the school-house. There would be school again tomorrow, and the next day, and the day after that.

Within a few minutes they were well away, trotting along a bare, narrow road. They walked for maybe two miles without exchanging a word. The sun had risen much higher in the sky by now and the boys sweated, their shirts sticking to their skin, dust and grit from the road clinging to their legs as they walked.

Cathal began to develop a stitch in his side. 'How far do you think it is from here?' he asked, slowing down as he waited for an answer.

'I don't know. We'll have to hitch a lift when we get to the Galway road. Someone will take us.'

When they got to the road it stretched out before them, thick and grey against the green landscape. It extended as far as the horizon, upon which was poised, they hoped, the blue expanse of the ocean. Clouds stacked themselves higher and higher in the sky and their shadows moved across the landscape like great ships cut adrift. Between the clouds the sky was a deep, fluid blue, the same colour as that of the sea in the picture painted in Cathal's mind.

He watched Hugh walking quickly in front of him, rummaging around in his pockets and retrieving every now and again the small, useless things that had collected there. He was a shambles, with his Ribena-stained shirt, worn pants above bruised, grazed legs, his hair sticking out at all angles. For Hugh, nothing seemed to matter beyond the moment he lived in; nothing had consequence.

He came from one of the poorest families in the parish. Their land was so damp that their chickens' feet had rotted and what few cows they possessed had picked up liver fluke from the sour meadow behind their house. Hugh's eldest brother, Niall, had studied for the priesthood in Drumcondra but had not taken his vows, deciding instead to take the boat to Liverpool where he now worked for a coal merchant. As Niall's first letter home was read out to the family, Hugh's grandfather had been heard to remark that one way or another Niall had been destined to end up wearing black.

The two boys walked on towards the horizon for a while before they heard a low humming increasing in the distance behind them. A small yellow car broke over a hump in the road about a half-mile away.

'Start waving now,' said Hugh, beginning to flail his arms wildly in the air.

They jumped up and down and waved as the car approached. Cathal swung his satchel round and round above his head. Hugh screamed out at the top of his voice.

The car slowed and came to a halt. Hugh ran to the passenger window as the driver leaned across to wind it down.

'Are you going to the sea?' he asked excitedly, and so loudly that the driver drew her head back.

She wore a sleeveless, faded black T-shirt and a cotton skirt the same colour yellow as the car. She pushed her dark sunglasses up into her hair as she went to speak.

'The sea?' she asked, as if she hadn't quite heard. She looked puzzled for a moment, her lips bunched together like a red carnation bud. 'If you want to go to the sea you're miles away.'

The two boys leaned in even closer to the car. 'We know,' Hugh said politely, 'that's why we need a lift.'

The woman looked out along the road for a few seconds. 'Well,' she said, 'I'm not going to the sea, but I can drop you close to it if you want.' She clicked open the door. 'Get in then.'

The car smelt of perfume, plastic and paint. Cathal sat in the back, next to a couple of trays of soft oil paint tubes and a large collapsible wooden easel. A bundle of brushes wrapped in damp newspaper rolled around the floor at his feet. Hugh sat in the front seat, chatting to the woman, who had introduced herself as Liz. She was from Athlone.

'What brings you out this way?' he asked, fiddling about with the lock on the glove compartment.

'I'm going out to Roundstone to do some more painting, and to get away from everything, I suppose.' She sounded exhausted.

She reminded Cathal of how his mother sounded on the mornings that she rose to get him out to school. Cathal looked at how her hair was pulled back in a tortoise-shell comb. He had seen one of these combs in a broken-handled mug upon his mother's dressing-table, but had never seen her wear it. The woman's shoulders were slumped, her eyes fixed upon the road ahead as if she could not see where she was going, but felt that it was the right direction.

As the car buzzed through the countryside Cathal read the labels on the paint tubes, some of which leaked in the pressing heat: Flesh, Burnt Umber, Magenta, Cyan, Canary Yellow, Charcoal Grey. With his thumb-nail he scooped a drip of the Flesh paint and smeared it along the back of his hand. The colour was completely different to that of his own olive skin.

Eventually the car drew to a halt at a crossroads. The woman pointed out a black and white road sign that read: TRA. Beneath they could see the impression of larger letters which had been crudely blacked out with dripping gloss paint.

'The beach is down there.' She leaned across Hugh and pointed down a narrow boreen.

While Hugh strained to look down the boreen the woman turned around to look back at Cathal for the first time. Through the tint of her sunglasses he could only see the curved reflection of the car's rear window. She smiled at him slowly and went to say something.

In that moment Cathal felt old, as old as his parents, as old as this woman, and as age-old as the common conflict which had somehow bound his life and hers together.

She said nothing. Cathal turned to look down the boreen as Hugh stepped out of the car. The woman pulled the passenger seat forward and Cathal got out.

'Goodbye, now,' she said softly, suddenly lifting her glasses from her eyes. They were deep brown with long, thick lashes and when she blinked there was a large freckle right in the middle of each unfolded eyelid, so that she would always seem to be looking at you, even with her eyes shut.

Cathal stared. 'Bye,' he said.

She closed the door after them. The bright sunlight caught on the chrome edging around the windscreen and leapt into his face. He turned away to clear the glare from behind his eyes and when he turned back the car was humming away up the road. He was sure that she was still watching him in the rear-view mirror.

Hugh was already some distance down the boreen.

'Come on, Cathal,' he yelled. 'Stop dreaming and come on.'

Cathal ran off down the gentle slope of the road. The sun

was at its highest by now and the heat rising from the road made Hugh's figure shimmer in front of him. The yellow gorse blossoms and the deep-green fuchsia leaves seemed to melt into the air along with the blue of Hugh's shirt. Cathal stopped a moment to allow the colours to separate in his eyes. He heard footsteps approaching from behind him but when he turned around there was nothing, just the dry-stone walls and clumps of ferns standing under the sun. In the distance the yellow car disappeared over the brow of a low hill. He ran ahead to catch up with Hugh.

They soon slowed to a walking pace, the heat too much for them, exhaustion beginning to contain their excitement. As they progressed further and further along the boreen they noticed silver sand tumbling in the breeze across the broken tarmac, and bunches of dried-out seaweed that snapped and crunched underfoot like dead leaves. Walking through the fields that stretched down to the coast Cathal noticed how the light that fell upon them seemed to be falling through water; a sub-aqueous light, bright and unforgiving. Everything here seemed exposed by it, drenched in it; pure.

'Let's run,' Hugh said, pointing to the summit of the nearest sand dune. 'It's just over here.'

Cathal, too tired to run any further, trudged through the sand watching his friend scramble up the back of the dune. He watched too as he saw Hugh's figure transformed into a black silhouette against the sky when he reached the crest of the dune.

Hugh came to a sudden and abrupt halt at the top of the dune. His arms dropped down to his sides. For what seemed like an age he stared out ahead of him, motionless against the deepening sky. When he turned his mouth was pursed shut, his arms swinging helplessly at his side. It looked as if his blank gaze was directed not at Cathal but into the heart of the landscape behind him, as if it was laughing at him.

'What's wrong?' Cathal called up to him. 'What can you see?' He quickened his pace now that he had seen Hugh's strange reaction. The sand filled his shoes before he reached the top where Hugh stood in silence. He grabbed Hugh's elbow for support and dragged himself upright, then raised his head and looked out to sea for the first time in his life.

There was nothing there. Stretched out before him, as far as the eye could see, was a solid ocean of sand. The tracks of birds' feet criss-crossed it at irregular intervals, but apart from this it looked plain and empty, as smooth as eggshell. In the distance to their right and left were dark ridges of naked rock jutting out towards the horizon, barely breaking the monotony.

A seagull swooped from nowhere, its long call screaming through the air. It landed on the slope of the dune below them and poked its smooth, angry head with its sharp eyes into a discarded soup can. The two boys listened in silence to the seagull's beak tap-tapping around the inside of the can as it foraged for scraps. Hugh turned away from the seagull and looked at Cathal who could only answer with a blank stare and then, after a moment, a shrug of his shoulders.

'What's happened,' asked Hugh, 'to the sea?' His mouth remained open after he had spoken. The breeze made a soft rushing, moaning sound as it blew across his parted lips.

'I . . . I don't know,' replied Cathal, his hands on his hips, surveying the unknown horizon. 'I don't know what to look for.'

'I've seen the sea before. I remember it from when I was young. I remember what it looked like; I *do*.' He stamped his foot down hard into the sand, then kicked a clump of grass out towards the soup can that the seagull had abandoned. 'The sea should be *here*.'

Hugh half-ran, half-tumbled down the slope to the thick band of stones and debris at the foot of the dune. Cathal waited at the top looking out at the horizon and then back behind him at the flat land with its dark turf-cut scars and winding stone walls. It all looked to him then as if the world was keeping something from him. He remembered what his father had told him two summers before, as he cut into the turf-bank with the *slean*. 'Don't believe a word anyone tells you, Cathal.' His words seemed forced out by the effort of cutting into the sodden ground. 'Wait, son, until you've seen it for yourself.' That day that the two of them had spent cutting turf was the first time that Cathal's mother had not walked the mile or so from the cottage with a flask of dark tea and brown bread sandwiches wrapped in a plastic bag. Cathal had spent the afternoon watching out for her whilst his father cut the turf as if there was nothing unusual going on, striking up sudden, short, unusual conversations about hurling, fishing and his old school in Tuam.

Cathal went down on to the beach where Hugh was poking around amongst the stones and broken sea shells. Hugh pulled at a half-buried lobster pot, the strands of brittle blue mesh tearing from the arched wooden struts and crumbling between his fingers. Not satisfied with this he placed his foot upon one of the proud struts and leaned down upon it. It splintered and cracked loudly, sending tiny insects flying from between its warped layers before snapping and bowing to the ground. He broke the remaining struts in the same way and soon the lobster pot was reduced to a jumble of wooden shards and torn netting. As they walked away the wind-borne sands began to colonise the destroyed remains.

The beach oozed water around their feet. Cathal stopped and took off his shoes so that he could walk barefoot, feel the grains of wet sand squeezing against his skin and sticking between his toes. Hugh crushed shells and dead crabs beneath his feet, dancing like a sprite from one victim to another.

Glancing out at the horizon, Cathal noticed that a thin blue line had appeared at the point where the seemingly eternal beach rose to meet the sky. When he looked again, a few minutes later, the thin line had grown to a solid band.

Hugh was kicking a large plastic drum across the stones.

'Come on!' shouted Hugh. 'Watch this.' He tossed the drum into the air and ducked as it fell back and cracked open on a large, sharp rock. His face filled with a curious delight as he danced across the sand.

Cathal followed Hugh at a slower pace, stooping to examine the crushed crab remains, their pale ribbed stomachs and smooth claws, jointed legs. The whorled surfaces of shell fragments caught his eye, and when he found one whole shell riddled with tiny holes he held it up against the sky. The holes were transformed into pricks of light, like stars in the night sky.

As he watched the blue thicken upon the horizon Cathal felt the breeze strengthening. It brought with it the taste of salt upon his lips, the smell of something strange in his nose. Now he saw how the fronds of seaweed caught on the foreshore pointed towards the horizon, how rivulets of wet sand ran from every rock, and how the crabs scuttled away from the land.

He found Hugh kneeling on the sand, bent over an object half-buried in the sand. It was a clear plastic bottle, wedged so that it stood almost upright, like a lighthouse of life amongst the stones and sand. He knelt down beside Hugh and peered inside.

A pair of bulging eyes stared back at the two boys. Behind these bulbous, rotating, fearful eyes was a set of distended, bleating gills, and beyond these the mottled body of a trapped rock-fish. It was much larger than the neck of the bottle and had probably swum in at one time, and then grown too large to escape. He watched the fish watching them before Hugh broke the silence.

'What'll we do with it?' he asked. He pushed at the plastic in front of the fish's head. It shirked away, a cloud of silt blooming in the water beneath its fins.

Cathal grasped Hugh's wrist. 'Leave it alone.'

'We could put it in a rock pool,' said Hugh, pointing at the line of dark, jagged rocks at the end of the beach.

'What if the bottle breaks, or we slip on the rocks? Just leave it where it is, Hugh.'

'No. It will die if we leave it here.'

Cathal sighed and looked down at the fish again. As Hugh began to scrape sand from around the bottle his hunched figure sent a shadow across the sand and Cathal remembered his father, or really his mother.

He remembered again the summer of two years before, the time that his father had really started drinking a lot, when he would rarely return from the town sober. He remembered the night that he had lain awake, listening out for the sound of his father's feet coming along the path to the cottage. But he had heard the sound of two pairs of feet and then whispering and giggling. A woman's voice. After a few more seconds he realised it wasn't his mother's. Cathal had gone to the window of his darkened bedroom and looked out.

On the path in front of the cottage he saw his father lying on top of Miss Toomey, the junior class teacher. His father's trousers were bunched around his knees and he could see the paleness of his buttocks as they rose and fell in the moonlight. One of his hands was pushed up underneath Miss Toomey's jumper and the other was outstretched, clutching a bottle of whiskey. Cathal watched them for a minute, his hands pressed against the cold glass. He heard Miss Toomey sighing and his father laughing out loud. Miss Toomey's hands ran up and down his father's back.

Cathal remembered the warm, unyielding mass of that same back as he had clung to it a few years before when his father used to pick him up and carry him piggy-back across the bog.

Just as his father pulled Miss Toomey's jumper up beneath her chin a light came on in the room next to Cathal's; his parents' bedroom. He pulled away from the glass but was still able to see his mother's shadow stretched out upon the grass in front of the house, framed by the curtains. She was standing quite still. The flood of light framed the bodies locked to each other on the path. Cathal strained to see them more clearly now. Miss Toomey's skin was almost albino white beneath his father's body. The new perm she had got during the Easter holidays was in a mess. Her breasts quivered and she rushed to conceal them with her hands, giggling nervously.

Cathal's father looked up at the figure standing in the window. His body seemed frozen. He slowly put the whiskey bottle to his lips and sucked a little as Miss Toomey laughed again. Then the light in the window went out as suddenly and as silently as it had come on.

Cathal looked out at the horizon. The blue out there was coming towards him. A cooler breeze began to blow across the sand, tugging at his shirt, tumbling fragments of dry seaweed across the sand and into the marram grass at the foot of the dunes. Clouds scudded across the sky a little faster than they had done earlier in the day. The drifting expanses of sunlight were smaller now on the distant mountains. Goosepimples appeared upon his skin.

An oyster-catcher settled on a nearby rock. Cathal watched it shaking its slender neck, its head held up to the sky like a sunflower. The breeze disturbed its feathers and it arched backwards to preen them back into place once again. After a while it lifted its wings and soared off over the sand dunes. He watched it disappear and then looked into the distance.

In the few minutes since he had last looked, the sky over the land had darkened. Now slate-grey rain clouds rolled across it. The Twelve Bens looked almost black, as if made of coal. And between the mountains and Cathal was the bog. Stretched like a blanket. The bog that concealed, and eventually offered up, the white bones of ancient creatures, the petrified stumps of drowned forests, and from time to time, the corpses of human beings; drowned, sucked into the black silt, sometimes thrown in.

The bog would conceal everything, for a while at least. And that concealment offered protection from the truth. Yet in time everything was revealed, everything offered up for inspection. Nothing could be hidden forever out here. Someone would see, someone would hear.

And still everything was trying to find a hiding-place. It was a land where donkeys made themselves small against the wind, where men worked unseen in turf-cuts. A land that young women drove to to escape their husbands before realising they could never escape themselves and that there was nowhere else to look out here but inside oneself.

It was a place where turf was never stacked more than a few feet high, where bog-roads led to nowhere, and where Cathal's father had had sex with a school-teacher on his own front path; not because he was drunk, but because in a land and a country like this it was as good a place as any to hide.

'Cathal! Cathal!' The shout burst through the air like a firework. There was no echo. There never could be in a land like this.

Cathal ran towards where Hugh was standing some way along the beach. As he neared him he saw that the bottle had broken. Hugh held one half of it in front of him, as far away from his body as possible, as if it was a moving, living thing. With his other hand he was pulling his shirt from his skin. A large, ragged brown stain spread out upon the shirt, and as he pulled a viscous fluid oozed through the thin cotton and dripped on to his bare legs. Tears came down his cheeks, dropping to make tiny hollows in the sand around his feet.

'What happened? What is that mess?'

'That bloody fish! The bottle broke and this stuff came out with the fish.' He pointed at the stain on his shirt.

Cathal looked behind Hugh and saw the dark wet patch amongst a cluster of stones. Hugh walked off across the beach towards the dunes. He did not look back.

Cathal knelt down to examine the remains of the fish. All that was distinguishable in the puddle of greenish-brown liquid was its head, tail, and fanned-out limbs. Its clouded eyes stared back at Cathal as they had done earlier from inside the bottle. Now they saw nothing, were frightened by nothing. As he watched, the remains diminished. The sand soaked the fish away until it was little more than a small stain of memory on the wide beach.

Hugh now stood at the foot of the dune over which they had first come. He waved, indicating that he was leaving.

'Wait!' shouted Cathal, breaking into a run. 'Look! The sea!' He swung his arm out towards the sea. The surf line was only a hundred yards away. Behind it a vivid blue mass of moving water.

'I don't care any more,' Hugh called back. 'I'm going home – this place is sick, and we're going to get killed when we get home.'

Cathal ran back across the stones to where Hugh stood shaking thick droplets of liquid from his shirt. There were dirty smears across his forearms and legs, and tracks down his cheeks from where his tears had run.

'Wait just a little longer, please,' said Cathal.

'No.'

'Please. I want to know what it feels like. I don't want to forget.'

'Forget what?'

'What finding the sea feels like.'

Hugh said no more. He began to walk back up the dune.

'Hugh,' said Cathal, the breeze tearing the word, hooping its soft sound in the air.

'Yeah?'

'What did you expect?'

Hugh paused for a moment, his back turned towards his friend, sliding the toe of his shoe across a large, surf-worn stone. He glanced back at Cathal and went to say something, but the words would not come. Soon he had disappeared over the dune. Cathal went back to the rock he had been sitting on earlier.

The tide surged in towards where he sat, lifting the remains of the crushed lobster pot on to its foaming surface. The stones' long, patient wait for the cool water was over. The dry seaweed regained its suppleness as the tide flowed across its stiff strands. The waves washed away the wreckage of the broken plastic drum. They dissolved the last traces of the sad fish, returning its blind eyes and redundant fins to the ocean depths, to where the currents would never flow, to where the water was as dark and still as a disused heart. The sea scoured the beach clean so that nothing, not even memories, clung.

Cathal watched over everything. There, above the wide

open ocean, he was content. He had found the sea. He savoured the rhythmical, inexorable toil of the waves that carried his heart away from what it had known before.

He reached into his school-bag and pulled out a tin whistle. Remembering the wedding photograph, he pulled it from between the two books and held it out upon his palm, waiting until the wind took it from him.

He allowed a thin stream of fine sand to run from the open end of the tin whistle. Then he looked across the ocean to the point where it seemed to join the sky. He closed his eyes, filled his cheeks, and began to play. The narrow notes slid out into the salt-washed evening, out over the sand, the drifting photograph, and out, out over the dissolving remains of the rock-fish, soaring upwards into the huge, clear air.

THE GUNFIGHTER

THE TWO VOLUNTEERS waited in silence. Occasionally one would look over at the other and catch a terror-struck eye. Even then no words of comfort or encouragement passed between them, just silence and the thick, clinging air of fear.

The narrow gravel road separating them led into the city. On either side of it were large, rolling sand dunes, covered in thick clumps of marram grass. Odd items of rusting machinery lay half-submerged in the soft sand at the side of the road and it was behind these brown, sinking hulks that the volunteers lay waiting for the British Army patrol they knew would come this way.

They heard the crunch of the soldiers' jack-boots moments before the patrol came over the brow of a dune. The four soldiers marched two-abreast with the sun upon the tender napes of their necks. The brass buttons on their tunics danced in the sunlight, spraying discs of shimmering light across the road. This did nothing to distract the attention of the two volunteers who had by now cocked their rifles and were sighting them upon those same sun-dancing brass buttons.

The reports of the first two shots were all but blown

across the dunes by the breeze. Two of the soldiers heard only the curious, dull cracking and splintering of their colleagues' breast-bones as the lead bullets carved their way through bone and gristle. Instinctively, they dropped to the ground behind the two dead men. The volunteers waited a few moments until the third soldier lifted his rifle from his shoulder and looked up to take aim. A single bullet caught him high on the forehead and the impact moment-arily lifted him into a kneeling position before his body slumped back to the ground. His colleague loosed off a volley of shots which ricocheted to safety along the centre of the road.

While the soldier re-loaded his rifle, Sean Hannan, the younger of the two volunteers, looked across at the other and smiled. Liam Curtin returned the smile, but signalled caution and patience before returning his gaze to a line along the barrel of his rifle. To his surprise a honey-bee had settled upon the gun-sight. He reached out and grabbed the bee with his hand. It beat frantically inside his fist, thumping tinily against his palms as he lifted it to his ear to listen to its buzz. He let it go when he heard the sudden rasp of a foot on gravel. A shot punctured the stillness and he swung his rifle around to fire in the direction of the British soldier. He could hear the frantic sound of running alongside him and fired twice in rapid succession. The running stopped and Liam pressed his face into the sand, listening.

'Sean!' he called out after a few moments. 'Sean!'

There was nothing; no answer, no sounds of movement. He looked up and saw that the body of the last British soldier lay face up in the middle of the road, his blind eyes staring at the passing clouds. Liam ran to where Sean lay crumpled in the gully at the side of the road. At first he thought the boy was only stunned but when he slapped his cheek Sean's head turned to reveal the gaping hole behind his ear. A dark crescent developed in the sand around his head; a halo of blood. Liam blessed himself and touched his fingers to the boy's lips. He leaned over and quickly prised Sean's fingers from the trigger of his gun. A good rifle was a valuable thing, and he could not leave it behind.

He crossed the road and pulled his bicycle from where it had been hidden in the soft, shallow sand. Leaping up on to the shiny leather saddle he glanced out over Dublin Bay, where a dark, rumbling thundercloud summoned its energy from the warm air.

I knew nothing of it then. He had telephoned me two nights before, asking me to come back to Ireland to see him. He wanted us all there, he said, he wanted us all to know. When I asked him to explain himself the line went dead. It was hardly surprising, coming from him.

I walked to the open bedroom window and looked down at the street below. The neon sign over the door of the liquor store across from our block blinked twice and died. The last tram made its way along the centre of the Avenue, flashes of blue where it caught the current from the overhead lines. Two dishevelled black men standing beneath a street-lamp shared a paper-wrapped bottle of bourbon. In the distance the skyscrapers stood emptied for the weekend, garlanded with cubes of light. Around me the city groaned, cloaked in humidity, moisture suspended in the air. These were the sights and sounds of an American city and in the morning I would tell my wife, Anna, that for a few days I would forsake them to return to my grandfather's house in Dublin for no better reason than he had asked me to.

The city smelled faintly of the pavements which had been freshly sprinkled with rain from a passing thunderstorm. O'Connell Street was awash with its usual plethora of people set against a pastiche of garish shop-fronts; a collision of colour. Lilting voices, mothers scolding grubby, chocolate-stained children, greasy hand-prints on Clery's windows.

I found a taxi which took me out along Mount Street towards the suburbs where I was born and where my grandfather now whittled his days away walking labradors on Sandymount Strand. The grotesque monotonous mortality of a man and his dogs set against a retreating tide; a life slipping away on a razor-shell-strewn beach; the marooned skull of an unfortunate Dalkey Island goat draped for death in seaweed, crabs for eyes.

Irene was at the house before me, heavy now with what would be my first nephew. Her awkward figure opened the door to me, the tendons flexing along her neck as she strained to kiss my cheek. The dogs yapped and barked at my feet, dribbling across my suitcase before deciding to follow me into the living-room where my grandfather languished at the fireside. The eyes in his balding, crenellate head turned to rest upon mine, a vivid red vein zig-zagging its way across the white of one eye.

'You are much too good to me, you know,' he said, shifting his weight in the deep armchair. 'I shouldn't have put any of you to all this trouble.'

'No trouble at all, Pops,' I replied. 'No trouble at all. It's good to see you looking so well.'

He exhaled loudly and phlegmatically through dry lips and turned his stare back towards the distorted reflection of himself to be found in the brass fireplace surround. He began muttering quietly to himself, indistinct words and syllables floating from his lips.

Irene tugged at my sleeve, beckoning me to come through to the kitchen. Following her, I saw that the sideboard was filled with warm, buttered scones and freshly-baked brown bread.

'He has slipped since I last saw him at Christmas,' I said. 'His spirit seems to have gone.'

'He has had it bad with his chest since March. Between the emphysema and the damp weather he's had a hard time of it.'

I looked around at the kitchen Irene had kept scrupulously clean. His trademarks were gone: the row of old pipes in the dresser, the small pot-cacti ranged along the windowsill, his boots standing beside the back door. He was being edged out slowly.

'He hardly had a word for me,' I said.

'He has little to say to any of us these days. Very little at all.' She whisked her hand around the water in the sink, retrieving potato-peelings which she dumped in the bin at her feet. 'I just leave him be.'

'You can't ignore him, Irene.'

'I *don't* ignore him.' She turned away from the sink and looked at me, water dripping from her reddened hands. 'You don't have to live with him.'

I felt uncomfortable at having questioned how she coped with him. It was true: I was at the periphery of the family now, with my American wife and sons. I had removed myself from his shadow.

A few minutes later she laid a mug of tea on the table in front of me. I thanked her for it and went to sit in the old rocking-chair at the window.

'Have you any idea why he wanted me to come all this way? He said he wanted us to know something. What?'

'I wish I knew, Eamonn, I really wish I knew,' she said. 'I suppose we'll get some sort of an explanation at dinner tomorrow evening. Siobhan can't come until then, so we'll hear nothing from him in the meantime.'

I turned to look out through the window at the garden. It looked so bedraggled now; Irene's sphere of influence had clearly not extended this far. The hedges were overgrown, the flower-beds bare, the roses pruned back into crude black stumps. The sundial that stood in the centre of the uncut lawn was now overrun with creeping ivy. No shadow had been cast upon its brass face for years. I remembered the days when all his hours were spent out there, tending to the climbing plants, the rockeries, the lawn, the shrubbery. Invariably there had been casualties: the prize clematis montana frozen to the downpipe the year that my parents were killed, the wallflowers crushed and petrified by a late fall of snow, the sleeping hedgehogs dragged out to die from exposure by labrador puppies.

Looking out at the state of the garden made me impatient with Irene and her smug school-teacher husband.

'Will you ever get around to mowing the lawn this year?' I asked. 'Just for his sake, of course.'

There was no reply. I turned around. Irene had slipped out while I had my back turned and the room was suddenly, violently empty. I felt uncomfortable in a room I had grown up in. I emptied the dregs of the milky tea into the sink.

Wandering back into the living-room I noticed that the old man was sleeping his troubled sleep. From time to time his hand would lift from the arm-rest as if he were about to say something and an expression would form upon his face; then his arm would drop and the expression fade. His hollow, aching wheeze blended with the roar the flames made in the hearth as they escaped up the chimney.

Little had changed in this room since the days when I had spent my evenings here poring over school exercises and the leather-bound collections of Shakespeare and Homer which still stood upon the bookshelves in the alcoves at either side of the hearth. The deep-green flock wallpaper had survived intact. At times it lent the room the look of a Fifties hotel lounge, with its large oak furniture and the lavishly upholstered chaise-longue beneath the window.

In the far corner the gun cabinet stood like a sentinel. The leaded glass in its doors had not dulled with age and cast my reflection back at me in a bluish haze. The large brass lock caught the lamplight. When I opened the cabinet door the light shifted and bounced off a mirror-topped coffee table and thence on to the crown of my grandfather's head. Intrigued, I watched it flicker there for a moment before looking into the dark interior of the cabinet. The acrid odour of metal polish mingled with the smell of leather filled my nostrils. Clearly, the old man had not neglected the rifles which had stood here since the Civil War had ended in the early 1920s. Indeed, it smelled as if they had been polished that very day, but that was unlikely.

From the fireside came a sudden, rasping cough. A gob of the old man's phlegm hit the fire-grate with a loud hiss. He mumbled a little and the armchair creaked while he settled back into it.

By the time I had returned to the kitchen Irene had fed the dogs. They dozed in a gloomy corner of the room.

'You must be tired after the long flight over,' she said, squeezing a floor-cloth between her hands. 'The jet-lag always catches up on you.'

Lethargy spread through me as I nodded agreement with her. I said goodnight.

'You're in your old room tonight,' she called up the stairs after I had gone.

I lay in bed staring at the ceiling rose for longer than I wished. I was remembering my grandfather as I had known him as a child; as I had known him before I had grown to know too much.

I remembered most of all how I had found him on the beach that August morning: standing still, naked, up to his knees in water, his eyes fixed upon a vanishing point in the distance, his heart set elsewhere. His brown jacket and trousers rolled in the foam at the edge of the surf. His shoes had already filled with sand. He had been standing there for some time, hesitating, caught between one life, one reality, and another he wished for.

'Pops! Pops!' I shouted, stepping high through the fizzing waves. He did not turn but bowed his head.

'Are you going for a swim?' I asked when I caught up with him.

He cupped his hands over his groin, like I had seen footballers do.

'Look,' he said simply, indicating with a nod the sea in front of us.

I looked. A series of sleek black humps broke through the water no more than a hundred yards away from us. They moved steadily across the bay.

'Porpoises,' he said, and we looked a little longer.

As we walked back through the water, gathering his drowned clothes, reclaiming the shoes, he stopped for a moment. I looked back at him, twisting his tie between my fingers.

'Some day you'll learn to forgive your granddad.'

His words made no sense to me.

Other moments in time slowly returned to me one after another, indexed as always by the internal music I invariably tagged to these stills of life: the fizz and bubble of the waves on a Connemara beach that morning as we stood entranced by a school of porpoises, the suck-plop of the peat bog from which my parents' car was pulled on a cold, misty October evening, the rattle of pebbles hitting coffin lids while their double grave was filled in, the insistent hum of the cardiac monitor attached to their driver as he lay on a hospital bed for days afterwards. Then, granddad talked only of his dogs.

Siobhan, the younger of my two sisters, arrived at noon the following day. She too had travelled some considerable distance in answer to the call from her grandfather.

'Hey, big brother!' It was her usual greeting. She had not lost many of her teenage habits and nuances. They were at once irritating and endearing. 'What's with the old man now?'

'Don't ask,' said Irene. 'Come into the kitchen for some tea. You're looking well.'

While they chatted in the kitchen I stood in the hallway

examining the photographs ranged along its walls. There was just one photograph of my parents, taken in the Botanic Gardens in Glasnevin during their last summer. My mother wore a long flowing pale dress and held a wide-brimmed hat on her head with one hand. Her chin was lifted up a little as she peered at the camera. My father stood beside her, feet apart, his hands pushed into the pockets of his trousers. His dark hair was oiled back, and beneath the pronounced eyebrows I had inherited from him, his hazel eyes stared hard into the lens.

I looked at the photograph more closely and noticed that at the edge of the print, beside my father, ran a narrow fraction of someone else's arm. Below that could be seen the edge of a shoe. It could have been no-one else but my grandfather. Someone had cropped the print so that he would not appear alongside my parents in the last photograph taken of them before they died. And yet, when I stepped back and looked at it again, those blurred pieces of sleeve and shoe were all that I could see.

Later, Siobhan and I exchanged news as we set out the table for the meal Irene had cooked for the four of us. I threw more coal on the fire and uncorked the wine. Together the three of us ferried the food from the kitchen to the dining-table.

'Come on, Pops,' said Siobhan, 'you'll burn up if you sit at that fire any longer.' She helped him up while Irene pulled a chair out from the head of the table for him. When he had sat down she hung his stick on the back of the chair.

His hands gripped the arm-rests as he leaned forward to look at us.

'Nice to see us all here, eating at the same table again,' he said, picking up his soup spoon.

'It's not that long since we were here last,' Siobhan commented.

He stirred the consommé with the spoon, blowing upon its surface to cool it down. The sound was that of a hoarse half-whisper as the air whistled around his loose dentures. Siobhan stared at him intently, a spoonful of soup suspended halfway between her bowl and her mouth. I glanced across at Irene, whose face seemed set, unperturbed. The whistling sound died down as he ran out of breath. Siobhan sighed and took her first spoonful of soup. I watched as he lifted the full spoonful to his lips and at the last moment noticed that Irene was wincing.

The gurgling, flooding sound that followed caused Siobhan to drop her spoon into her bowl. Irene was still wincing, and her shoulders shook a little. I noticed that as he ate his eyes were closed and his face took on an expression of ecstasy and anticipation; the face of a child being given a sweet cough mixture. Much of the soup spilled back out of his mouth and into his bowl or down his chin. As he breathed out after each swallow, droplets of consommé leapt from his lips into the air. I could not be sure that Irene hadn't planned it this way: serving soup to demonstrate how difficult he had made life for her and that Siobhan and I should be grateful to her for taking him on.

'So little has changed since we had dinner at this table every Sunday evening years ago,' I said as soon as he had finished his soup. I hoped to dispel the atmosphere that his soup-eating had fostered.

'That's true, Eamonn. It's a pity the chance won't come around again,' he said.

'Don't be daft!' Irene exclaimed. 'We'll all be here again at Christmas, won't we?' She looked at Siobhan and me.

'Not,' I thought, 'if we're going to have soup again.'

Siobhan remained silent, looking into space. I imagined that at that moment she wanted desperately to be back in London, to be away from us all, away from the grandfather who disgusted her so much.

'Won't we?' Irene repeated, louder this time.

I nodded. Siobhan woke from her day-dream and agreed.

'I think this chest of mine will get the better of me before then,' Pops said, adding a violent cough to emphasise his point.

'Nonsense,' said Irene, picking the empty soup bowls off the table and bringing them back to the kitchen.

While Irene filled our plates with meat and vegetables we talked about Siobhan's career and the changes in the school curriculum which meant that Irene's husband had had to change schools. Although we tried to engage him in conversation Pops would not talk.

When he went to cut his meat the knife wobbled between his fingers and then, as he ate, most of the food fell from the fork on to his plate. He chewed the tiny morsels with exaggerated effort and Siobhan kept her eyes upon her own plate and the label on the wine bottle in front of her.

'This talk of your chest getting you down is rubbish, and I won't hear of it,' said Irene. 'The Black and Tans couldn't nail you during the Civil War and it'll take more than a bad cough to get you down for too long.'

I leaned across to top up his glass in encouragement even though he had not touched his wine.

'Irene's right, you know.' I poured wine into his glass until he reached out and tapped the back of my hand. 'Every one was afraid of the Black and Tans, Pops, and you stood up to them.'

He poked wearily at his food, clearly not wanting to eat but not wishing to offend Irene either. He swallowed slowly, then went to speak.

'The first time I ever saw the Black and Tans coming down the main street in our town I ran and hid in the cellar of my uncle's pub. The whole town knew that they were only coming to give a couple of the local lads a hiding, and I was nowhere to be found for hours. Who would call that brave, eh? Sure, those bastards put the fear of God into me.'

'But weren't you one of those who ran them out of the town a week later? You've told us often enough that the street was thick with British blood afterwards.'

'I was there all right, but I have neither the spirit nor the will now that I had then,' he said, and after a time added, 'I'm a different man now.'

'Listen, Pops,' Irene began, 'don't start trading sympathies with us. You spent enough time talking about the Civil War to convince us you were a one-man army. You have a reputation to live up to now.' She smiled, clearly hoping that the jibe would humour him.

He scowled. A lump of half-chewed beef rolled off his bottom lip and dropped into his plate. 'I've a different mind on all that now.' He turned his head to cough. 'I can't rely on memories to keep the dream alive. Look at the state of The North now! A bloody mess is what it is!' He began to cough loudly and I patted his back as his face reddened. 'I should have buried the memories long ago,' he continued after a while. 'It's the likes of me that have created the myth that those thugs in The North live by. They look upon me as a hero, a great patriot. They don't know the half of it.'

'There's no need for any of that, Pops,' I said, 'what's done is done. You did what was right at the time.'

'It's not done, Eamonn, it's not done yet. It's still going on up there, and the fact that I did it sixty years ago makes me no different from the lot of them. They say that it was us that brought about the Republic. Huh! All those deaths, executions, widows and orphans. And for what? A freedom achieved years afterwards of its own will. It would have happened anyway, without the likes of me murdering Englishmen.' He set his cutlery down on the edge of his plate with a soft clink. 'Or Irishmen for that matter.'

The room was suddenly enveloped in a thick silence that was hardly silence at all. Each of us was looking for a way out of it. We stopped eating, stopped chewing. Siobhan swallowed hard and although she stared at the wine label even more intently than before, I knew that she too was listening out. Irene brushed the palms of her hands with a napkin, her mouth set fast, her lips bunched together. Darkness stood outside the window behind his head, twitching with curiosity. Moths streaked through it.

In the end it was he that defused it: 'I am thinking of young Sean Hannan. Seventeen he was, seventeen.' He paused to sigh. His sombre tone was infectious, viral – darkness seemed to creep in and take its place at our table. 'I am thinking of him now, thinking of what he would have become had he lived, thinking of the family he would have had and the lives they too would have lived.'

'Well!' Irene interrupted, 'I have never heard such rubbish coming from a grown man in all my born days!'

He ignored her and continued in the same sad, prosaic tone as before: 'I am thinking of the day that he died. Is it really sixty years? It was a day not unlike this one, you know. Dull, cloudy; thunderstorms rolling around the sky like demented ghosts. *He* should have lived to see another day – not I.' He coughed, turning away from the table to cup a hand over his mouth. I caught the gleam of a tear gathering in the corner of his eye.

Irene took the opportunity to interrupt again. 'Sean Hannan was killed by a British bullet and that's all there is to it. Sure isn't that his rifle in the cabinet over there along with your own?'

We looked over at the cabinet while he drew a long breath. I felt his hand upon my forearm. He tightened his grip and asked me: 'Will you fetch me his rifle?'

Under protest from Irene I took the rifle from its resting-place and brought it to him. He took it in his gnarled hands, running a finger along the smooth length of the barrel. Examining it, he said, 'I am tired of thinking of him now, tired of being like this. Those thoughts have me trapped now, locked away by what might and could have been. It should have been me, lying at the side of the road that morning.'

'We understand how you must feel,' Siobhan said calmly, 'but there's no need to burden yourself with blame at this stage. No one else blames you.'

'No one else knows the truth, that's why.' He shifted the rifle from one hand to the other.

I looked at my sisters and then turned my gaze towards him.

'Don't any of you see what I'm trying to say?' His voice faltered. 'I . . .'

'Now, now, Pops,' said Irene, 'that's no way to be acting on a night like this. Just forget about this whole thing. Eat your dinner and be thankful for the life you *have* got. And would you ever put away that monstrosity of a gun – it's making me nervous.'

'Let him say what he has to say,' I snapped. I tapped his shoulder. 'Go on, Pops.'

He looked at me and I could see that he was grateful for

the opportunity to talk without interruption. He quivered with nerves and faltered on his first words. 'F . . . Forgive me for all this trouble, calling you over here. It wasn't without good reason.' He leaned forward and propped his head up with his hand at his temple. His fingers were long and liver-mottled against his forehead. His eyes were fixed upon the carpet at his feet, as if he was concentrating upon words travelling a great distance. 'I regret . . . no . . . I have never forgiven myself for your parents' death. I lost more than a son and daughter-in-law in the crash. It was an accident, you know that. But I had my mind on other things as we drove back from the hotel that night. I was thinking of the laughs we had had at the party and your mother was re-telling some of the stories we had heard. The three of us were laughing away until I caught sight of myself in the rear-view mirror.' He lifted his head for a moment and looked at us before continuing. 'I saw myself smiling away without a care in the world, laughing with your parents, happy to be there. And then I thought of that young boy who could not be there – that young boy whose absence from the world is my fault.'

His elbow slid forward across the table and his head dropped towards the polished teak surface. I grabbed his wrist and pulled him upright. I could hear Irene and Siobhan cursing behind me. He drew himself upright with sudden strength. Pushing his face close to mine I could smell the sourness in his breath.

'I killed him, by God! I killed the poor boy. He got in

the way and I killed him.' He was frantic now, grabbing for my clothes, trying to pull me close. A wine glass toppled over and sent its contents splashing across the table-cloth. I steadied him, his words racing through my mind as I worked to comprehend them.

'Well!' Irene stood up from the table, wiping wine from her blouse.

He was sobbing by now. A loud, buckling sobbing that bore the unmistakable ache of years. I took the rifle from where it had fallen across his lap and laid it down upon the floor. Now it seemed almost impossibly heavy.

Irene stood at the door. Siobhan held her head in her hands, wine dripping from the edge of the table and on to her bare knee.

I leaned over him, grasping his shoulders in some half-futile attempt to comfort him in his desolation. Beyond the window the moths were hysterical now, blurring together in the pitch blackness, desperate, struggling for the light.

TRAIN ABOVE THE CITY

NOTHING CAN HAPPEN again. This is the truth and in time I must learn to accept it. For now though, it is hard to bear, and harder still to understand.

I stepped down from the bus and stood for a moment on the oil-speckled concrete floor of the bus station. A few other men brushed past me, anxious to dissolve themselves into the city. I followed their path towards the ticket hall. Inside, a group of three men stood around a coffee machine in a far corner, sucking on thin cigarettes, coughing and wheezing as I approched them. When I asked where I could catch a bus to the west of the city, they merely lifted their heads and looked at one another before shaking their heads in unison. As soon as I walked away they began muttering to each other and rocking back and forth on their heels, the cigarettes now discarded, their arms folded across their chests.

The ticket office was closed and the back page of *The Irish Press* taped across the glass prevented me from seeing if any of the staff were about. A door swung open behind me and I turned to see the bus driver emerging from the toilets, still doing up his flies. I thought of asking him if he knew where to find a westbound bus but he did not look the communicative type.

Outside the station I followed the smell of the river down to the quays. I looked downstream at the rising disc of the sun which seemed to stare out across the city, draping a diffuse light across the pavements and rooftops, brightening the dull copper domes of the buildings that lined the river. The light began to settle slowly upon everything it could find, as if it were a multitude of invisible hands reaching out through the darkest alleyways and into the deepest shadows that lingered behind the gasometer across the river from where I stood.

The tide was filling. The waters were like me, returning after a long, enforced absence. And even as I watched, the river was transformed, alloyed, into a bright ribbon of liquid metal, sliding silently through the dark, soot-blackened heart of the city.

I turned away and walked eastward into the sun. Far, far ahead of me I could make out the shape of the Liverpool ferry turning into its dock on the North Wall, a dark indistinct blur almost swallowed by the intensity of the sunlight. Everything was returning to this city.

I walked without meeting a soul for maybe a mile. I relished the freedom of walking such a distance in a straight line, feeling my legs stretch out after the confinement of the bus journey. I reached a night-watchman's hut and went to turn back the way I had come. The walls of the hut were peppered with woodworm holes and moss grew in the damp crevices between the slats of wood. I looked at it for a moment before noticing the *Miranda Guinness*, slipping upstream on the incoming tide, its bow barely breaking the surface. As I turned back I remembered.

'A move west,' she had said during her last telephone call. 'A move west and away from all that Kilbarrack crap.'

The bitterness in her words was unmistakable. She said that none of the neighbours had called around to say goodbye on the day that she left the first-floor flat in Larkin Crescent which she had lived in since two days after we were married. She said she had turned around and spat upon the doorstep before bundling our two daughters, Susan and Helen, into the waiting taxi.

I looked up along the river as far as I could see, past O'Connell Bridge, past the Ha'penny Bridge, to a point just beyond Christchurch where the banks of the river merged into a dull mass of grey and yellow. I could hardly imagine what the city looked like beyond that point. I had heard about the new housing estates out there, in Chapelizod and Lucan, Swords and Naas; but for me they were anonymous, colourless. Now my wife and children had moved there in my absence.

As I walked back along the quays a few cars passed along the road next to me, threading their way into the city from the ferry I had seen docking earlier. I came up alongside a small car that had stopped to let a truck pull out from a side road. A red-haired woman in the passenger seat plucked idly at the bra strap which crossed her shoulder. The sight of her bare flesh as she shifted it to and fro along her shoulder transfixed me. I watched as she tugged at the collar of her blouse and exposed a constellation of pale red freckles that worked their way across her back.

It was so long since I had seen a woman's body, so long since I had smelled a woman's scent. I did not think of Karen then, but of a teenage prostitute whom I once had sex with in a doorway behind Jervis Street Hospital. She, unwashed and sweating a little as she bared her thin body to me, smelled more human than anyone else I have ever encountered. Her smell has stayed with me all these years.

To dispel the longing that was rising inside me I walked to the edge of the quay and looked down at the water. It slapped rhythmically against the quayside, battering the green-slimed stone walls, returning the distorted reflection of my pink, distant face and a blue sky above.

The first time that I ever struck Karen was like waking up from a dream. Just as the first note of a thin scream escaped from her open mouth I stopped still, the wooden clothes brush still in my raised fist, its imprint already a grape-coloured stain upon her cheek. She scrambled away from me along the floor and I ran after her. In my horror I had pulled her out of the house and locked her in the boot of the car. During the drive to the hospital I had to turn up the radio to drown out her screams. The nurse in the casualty ward eyed me with derision as her slim, clean fingers prodded Karen's cheekbone. I could do nothing but stare at my hands, at my face in the mirror, not for a moment believing that I could have done this to someone I loved.

Across the city the light was still changing; the sky, the colours it would wear for this day, undecided. People appeared upon the grey pavements as if from nowhere, running in front of cars and students' bicycles, collars pulled up and chins down against the early-morning chill. There were dogs too, and young people with suitcases heading for the train station and the bus terminus I had left behind. Slowly the city was pulling together its fragmented parts, like a painter arranging the colours upon his palette before embarking on a new work. I had not seen these streets and walls in six years. Six years spent within the walls of a Midlands prison, with nothing but the streets of the heart to explore.

My mother's memory filled those hard, echoing streets, and I find it difficult to understand why it too has stayed with me all these years. Perhaps it is the very poverty of that memory that has caused me to cling to it.

I remember sitting in my uncle's study with a small, neatly-packed suitcase against the wall, my legs swinging over the edge of the armchair without touching the floor. I held three fairground tickets between both hands. In the kitchen behind me my aunt was shouting at my uncle. I heard my mother's name mentioned every now and again.

My uncle was saying nothing. Instead, when he got angry, my uncle had a habit of lifting objects from where they stood and replacing them with a tiny, dull thud. There were a lot of things for him to lift and replace in the kitchen.

I heard the sound of heels on the front path and my aunt stopped shouting. My uncle went on lifting and replacing things for another few seconds. He would always have the last word.

My mother's soft Antrim accent came to me like forgotten music, and then she was in the room pulling me up to her, pushing my face against her neck. But her perfume was new, unfamiliar, and there were sad tears in her eyes.

At the fairground in Booterstown my mother held my suitcase and walked behind me, talking to my aunt. I kept turning around to look at her as if she was my prize possession. She smiled back. At the Ferris Wheel she took the candy floss from my hand and strapped me into one of the seats. She dropped two coins into the breast pocket of my jacket and kissed my forehead. I pleaded with her to get in with me but she said she was afraid of heights. The wheel moved off with a shudder and I waved at her, feeling my heart begin to rise inside me as I went ever higher and higher. When I looked down I saw my mother hand the suitcase and candy floss to my aunt then turn away towards the entrance gate. My aunt would not look at her as she walked away. I began to call after her, again and again, my chest straining against the straps, tears upon my cheeks.

Eventually she was gone. Far below me, my aunt was picking holes in the puffs of candy floss.

As I walked westward, into the heart of the city, I thought about Karen's life with our daughters out there in Chapelizod. I wondered what colour the rooms of the new flat were, how it was wired (I used to be an electrician), and whether it looked out on to a yard or a garden. I wondered, too, about what shops Karen visited, what her neighbours were like and whether she told them that I was in prison because six years ago I had taken a hammer to her fingers.

In truth I knew nothing of her life, only her past, our past. I could not remember what class my daughters were in at school, nor what year they had made their First Communion. I could not remember the perfume Karen wore.

At the telephone box I hesitated before picking up the handset.

'Karen,' I said quietly when she answered my call.

I heard her gasp and there was a pause.

'Karen,' I said again.

'Joe?'

'They've let me out a day early. They need the cell. I'm in the city centre now, love.' I could hear my voice trembling with excitement and relief. I leaned over to rest my forehead against a glass panel in the side of the telephone box. Its coolness allowed me to steady myself.

'Don't send the girls to school today. Bring them in here to meet me.'

There was a long, empty silence before she spoke.

'Joe,' she said, 'they're gone already. They go to swimming lessons on Thursday mornings now.'

'You never told me.'

'I can't tell you everything.'

'We can both meet them after school then.'

'No, Joe, we won't. They haven't seen you in almost six years. It's a long time, and they're still frightened.'

Each word hurt like a small, cold stab. Frightened, she had said, my own daughters were frightened of me. I gripped the handset so hard that the colour left my knuckles. I felt something rising slowly inside me, like water drawn to the surface of an aquifer. I wanted to put the phone down, walk away, and bury what I was feeling beneath the city's pavements.

The pane of glass broke into a multitude of tiny, translucent cubes as I forced the handset through it, splashing out on to the street. People stopped to look over at me, pointing down at the constellation of glass fragments on the pavement, exchanging a few words among themselves. They began to turn away. In each of their faces I caught half-remembered fragments of my mother's features: delicately-ribbed lips, hazel eyes, the line of her neck, that shell-like whorl of her ear. When they turned it was my mother's back I was seeing and not the backs of unknown pedestrians.

As I stared down at my hands I heard Karen's voice crackling from where the handset swung intact. At first her words were indistinct but slowly things came back to me and I went to speak, leaning against the coin-box for support.

'Karen?'

'What has happened there?' She was practically shouting, hysterical now, words spilling from her lips.

'Nothing,' I mumbled. 'I dropped the phone, that's all.'

It was some time before either of us spoke again. Instead of talking, for talking would have done no good then, we listened to the sounds of our mutual silences, remembering the circumstances in which these taut silences had occurred before.

'Joe,' she began after a few minutes, 'don't come around here just yet. Go for a walk. Think about things and then we'll meet later on.' She paused. 'You know something, Joe?' she sighed. 'We are happy with our lives now.'

Throughout the day, as I walked the streets of the city, looking forward to the evening when I would meet my family at the train station, people seemed to come and go like swarms of insects. Sometimes they would appear like the first fractions of a great, hidden multitude; a locust swarm. At other times the streets would empty in the blinking of an eye, as though the people had merged with the city to become the stone pillars of the University, the Custom House, the Bank. At these times I became acutely aware of my presence among them. My footfall seemed the loudest of them all, my clothes the most distinctive, my hair the most closely-cropped. I seemed to catch the eyes of every face that walked past me. It was as if they recognised something about me; not my face, I felt, but my crime. They seemed to shy away as I approached; knowing me to be a wife-beater, a man who once picked up a hammer and, one by one, broke the fingers of the woman he loved most.

Yet I knew that this was untrue, that not one of them knew what I was capable of. None of those people could have seen how history had disfigured me. What I knew was that as these people vanished from the streets, enmeshed in their own lives and loves, they would never be heard of again.

And now, on this train above the city, they are all around me. As I sit next to a cracked window, they are unfolding newspapers and lighting cigarettes, talking in low, unsteady murmurs. A few are staring at the floor, and others, like me, are looking out of the window. They are watching the elements of the city slide past in the half-light. They are watching the city replenishing itself in their wake, watching the light failing across the roof-tops just as it constantly fails across every roof-top, in every city, after every day.

The train moves slowly, cautiously, as though it is feeling its way along the cold steel tracks, as though it knows it is taking each of us into our futures, some known, some

unknown. As it moves my mind is moving with it, threading its way back through my life, like a bee tracing its
invisible way back to the hive. Memory moves through the
years of my life, stopping here and there before moving on,
and on, gathering as it goes. It feasts on experience, embel-
lishing the truth, fleshing out those half-remembered
events with fantasy and lies. It is weighing itself down. The
train is taking me to where my wife and daughters are
waiting. I sit here at this window so that I can see them as
I approach.

There they are. Karen is unmistakable as she crouches
down to straighten the hem on Helen's dress. A breeze
spills strands of hair across her face, some of which catch
upon her lips. Susan reaches up and pulls them away. Both
girls have grown. They wear clothes I do not recognise.
Helen wears her hair in a bob now. Susan's is shoulder-
length, like her mother's. Karen looks across at the train but
does not notice me even though I have my face pressed
against the cracked window. There is a distance in her eyes
which I do not recognise, but understand.

I close my eyes and feel my heart beating harder and
harder. To have them in my arms, the sound of their voices
in my ears, their smell in the air around me, the warmth of
their presence. It is deep within the intensity of moments
like this that I see most clearly how I have not changed in
six years. I open my eyes and pretend that I have seen
nothing more than my wife and daughters waiting for me
across a railway track. I pretend that I do not exist.

People are stepping off the train. Their footfall resonates beneath the steel and glass arch of the station canopy. I want to follow them, allow my footfall to become theirs and walk to where my family wait for me.

I cannot. Instead I will stay here on this train and watch that future slide past me, dissolving in the light over the city; failing as it has always been failing. I will stay on this train that leads to the ferry terminal. I will leave them to live the life that they are happy with, where nothing will happen again.

The train is moving once again and still the memories fall back upon me. They swarm in; a flurry of burdened insects. I will dismiss them as with the briefest swipe of my hand I dismiss the patch of my breath condensed upon the cracked glass window. They are nothing but the ghosts of the past, exploring the present.

LIFE LINES

NOTHING SEEMED ABLE to settle into the room. A cat moved anxiously around the margins, looking for somewhere to lay itself down. At the window a large blue-bottle fly tapped repeatedly against the glass. Even the light thrown out by three large oil lamps seemed unsure of its function: too strong one moment, too weak the next.

Helen watched her mother bend down in front of the fire to riddle the grate. She put her hands to her ears as metal scraped across metal. The pile of embers settled lower and gradually glowed brighter.

'There,' her mother said, spreading her palms out towards the rejuvenated heat, 'that's much better.'

Helen put down the magazine she had been reading and stared into the flames for a while, watching them flicker, the shapes constantly changing. She seemed lost in their movement for some time. Every so often she looked across at her mother who sat at the end of the deal table sorting the contents of a wooden sewing-box. Her mouth puckered and her eyes strained with the effort of matching buttons, needles and threads in the uncertain light. Helen's eyes travelled back and forth from the magazine to her mother's face, monitoring her mood.

'Mam,' she ventured as soon as she noticed the slightest intimation of a smile upon her mother's lips.

'Yes?'

'Oh, nothing.' Helen turned back to the magazine.

Her mother closed the lid of the sewing-box with a firm snap and looked over at Helen. 'What's troubling you now?'

Helen set the magazine down on her lap, her face reddening. She heard her mother's breathing, soft and shallow. 'I went down to the post office today to collect something I've been expecting for a few days now.'

'We all know that,' her mother interrupted.

'Who knows?' Helen felt her throat tighten in panic.

'Your cousin Michael saw you down there at the crack of dawn. He tells me that the letter that came for you had an English stamp on it, and Father Duggan said that it was a London postmark. Is this true?'

'Yes, it is.' She lifted her head to look at her mother's dark, bead-like eyes. 'It did come from London. It had the news I wanted to hear as well. They're going to offer me a place as a trainee nurse in a teaching hospital over there. Isn't that wonderful, Mam? Isn't it?' She blurted the words out in one nervous breath so that her mother had to mouth them back to herself so as to fully comprehend them.

'Well,' she said, eventually. 'Well, well, well,' she repeated, almost to herself. She laid one hand across the other on top of the sewing-box and smiled back at Helen, her small eyes brightening. 'That's a start now, isn't it?'

Helen stood up, the magazine sliding across her knee, and went over to her mother who took her in her arms and hugged her.

'It is, Mam, it is.'

She breathed in hard and smelled her mother's thick scent. Her mother's smell was almost indistinguishable from the smell of the house around them. It was the smell of a woman married at twenty and with seven children by her thirty-fifth year. It was the smell of a woman who served the household she bound together.

And as she breathed in that smell Helen believed that such a life would never be hers, that she would become a woman in her own right, with an existence all of her own.

Around her the room was so utterly familiar. Nothing seemed to change. The sewing-box, its wood blackened with the prints of too many needle-pricked thumbs. The bowl of raspberries on the counter. A snapped stem of fuchsia pushed into a glass jug beside the sink. Even her mother's embrace was stale with age and too-casual repetition.

'It's a real start,' her mother said in the silence that had developed. She had begun to sense her daughter's anxiety, her unease prowling the room. 'Jarlath . . .' she faltered.

Helen moved away, tweaking a lip between her teeth. Her mother sought out her daughter's eyes with her own, looking to reassure.

She had avoided meeting him for the past few days, but he was never far from her thoughts.

'I'll tell him soon enough.'

'How?'

'I have my ways with him. I'll tell him in my own good time.' She trembled, almost a visible shaking.

The cat scratched at the foot of the door, its mouth blood-red in the blackness of the doorway. Helen went to let it out, and stood upon the doorstep for a while afterwards, looking across the bay where seaweed moved beneath the still surface of the water like drowned hair. The thick scent of honeysuckle in the August evening was almost too rich, too sweet upon her tongue.

The strand curved around and away from the harbour like a bright, sharp sickle lying in the cup of the bay. Beyond it stood the dark, forbidding hill that gave the area its name: Duindubh. Poised on top of the hill were the ruined remains of an ancient fortress, its empty windows staring out to sea like a blind watchman. A breeze tugged small clouds across the blue sky but their shadows never showed against the black flanks of the hill.

The same breeze tugged at Helen's thick linen skirt as she sat on the harbour wall watching the men in the boats below stringing marker-buoys to lobster pots. There had been times when she would have sat there all day, happy just to watch the men work before returning to the house to help with the dinner for her father and the younger children. Now she was impatient, her heels swinging back against the wall, her restless fingers picking at the loose threads in her jumper.

Jarlath stood amidst the men in the wooden boats, hoisting crates of fresh lobsters up on to the pier. He worked like a human machine, completely absorbed in his task. His thick, powerful arms lifted crate after crate with the same rhythmic effortless motion. She watched as the lobsters' heavy claws snapped at the air and their tails slapped the bottom of the crates.

She went down the slipway towards him. Oil-slicked water lapped the stonework at her feet and the shattered, discarded shells of crabs were everywhere; floating in the water, caught in strands of seaweed, littering the flagstones, their countless destructions woven into the fabric of the little harbour. She stood watching the men work for a minute or two before one of them caught sight of her and tugged at Jarlath's sleeve.

As his face turned towards hers Helen decided that she would have to tell him as soon as possible, that very day. To leave it any longer was to deceive him, and to prolong her own pain, and fear. Yet when her face met his it seemed that there was little need to say anything at all.

She watched him step through the boat, sending it rocking from side to side, the other men cursing him beneath their breath as they struggled to keep their balance. As he waded through the shallow water towards her she tensed and folded her arms across her breasts. There was something in his eyes already and she closed her own so that she would not see it.

His lips brushed along her cheek like a child's touch

before he turned her away from the sea, away from the distant horizon she longed for, and back towards the land she knew too well. They walked back up the slipway, his broad hand resting in the small of her back, guiding her through the stacked lobster pots.

His boots oozed seawater and she told him to change them as soon as he got home so that the wet leather would not chafe his feet.

'Never mind that,' he said softly. 'What brings you down here this early?' His words seemed to float in the air like prayers. He broke away from her and pulled a lobster from one of the crates around them. Although its claws were tied together with string its tail bucked forcefully as he swung it free of its companions. 'Why this early?'

Her silence stretched out before them like the path they walked along, naked and empty. She knew she could hide it from him no longer.

'Jarlath,' she said, leaning her head into his shoulder, remembering what she had prepared for this moment. 'I'm going away for a while. I'm going to train as a nurse . . . in London.'

He stopped walking and she stepped a little ahead of him before stopping herself. His eyes were still fixed along the path in front, as if he had not heard her.

'Jarlath . . . ?'

There was a loud cracking, splitting noise as Jarlath burst the lobster open with a simple, solitary squeeze of his hand. Pieces of red-purple shell exploded from it, soft flesh and fluids spilling from between his fingers. The lobster's wandering antennae flicked around once more and were still. He dropped it to the ground and shook its remains from his hand.

'When did you get this idea into your head?' He stood before her, his ribbed and veined hands resting upon his belt.

When he crushed the lobster Helen had stepped away from him, but she thought better of it now and reclaimed the distance. 'I sent away the month before last.' Her words stumbled from her mouth. 'I . . . I thought that nothing would come of it. It was just a shot in the dark.' The uncertainty of her speech did little to conceal the underlying intent.

'You don't have to go,' he said, 'there's plenty for you to be doing here in Duindubh. The house needs looking after and your brothers and sisters, what'll they do if you leave?'

'They're well able to look after themselves, and the house too if they have the will to do it.' She had regained her confidence now and the words came to her more easily than she had hoped.

'You've been here all your life.'

'I'm only nineteen, Jarlath. I'm still at the beginning of my life.' She looked out across the bay to where two men were leaning out of a currach dropping spider crabs into a floating cage. It was something she had seen them do almost every day for the past nineteen years. 'London will be a new life for me.'

Jarlath followed her gaze out towards the bobbing currach. He recognised the Conneely brothers and they him,
but he did not acknowledge their wave. A faint thud
carried over the water when they dropped the lid of the
cage shut and pushed away towards the harbour wall.
When he turned back he saw Helen's eyes fastened upon
the remains of the lobster and moved to block her line of
sight.

'Jarlath . . .' she began, but the words left her. Her confidence was waning. She searched for something else to say,
but could find nothing to offer him. 'You could come with
me to London,' she blurted. 'There's plenty of work on the
sites, and you could stay with that cousin of yours in
Kentish Town.' But it was not what she wanted and he was
not to be deceived now.

'This is where I belong.' The sentence slid softly from
between his lips and coiled itself in the air between them,
like an invisible spring.

She knew there was no answer. He did belong in Duindubh. His father and his father before him had been lobster
fishermen. It sang in their blood, in the air they breathed.
Now that his father's health was failing it would be for
Jarlath to take the helm on the family boat, it would be for
him to decide whether they would put to sea before any
storm could claim the pots, and it would be he that
negotiated a price with the wholesalers. It was his birth-
right and he would not have it taken from him.

'This is where I belong,' he repeated, tightening the

spring. He looked up and went on down the harbour path, past the up-turned currachs and the burnt-out shell of the kelp house.

Helen put her hands to her face for a moment then went after him, walking a few paces behind, towards the clutch of houses clinging to the lower-most slopes of the hill.

His house was no more than a few hundred yards from hers and he could watch her from his bedroom window as she made her way up towards her front door. She turned to look out to sea. Her skirt blew around her ankles and the breeze caught her brown hair and spread it across her face. She had her father's heavy jaw and her mother's large grey eyes that people said were only pretty when she smiled. He had heard others call her plain, but he saw beauty in her every movement.

She went inside, the door closing slowly behind her. Jarlath put his palm flat against the window and pressed until his knuckles shone white against the glass. He brought his other hand down hard upon the wooden windowsill and felt the impact reverberate through the glass. He was angry with himself at not having shown her to her door like he had always done, or at not asking her in for tea when they had passed the track that led to his house. He had been too angry to say anything while she told him of the arrangements her parents had made for her journey to Dublin and then to London. He knew that his anger counted for nothing in all of this. It was done now.

He had tried to keep his gaze from her as they walked, so that he would not see his dreams reflected in her eyes, in her skin. Those dreams, so carefully constructed over a period of months that had begun to stretch into years, seemed empty and hollow now; worthless things.

Helen's younger sisters and brothers sat together on the sand, well away from the bonfire. Other families gathered around them. Their black shapes moved against the flames, passing foil-wrapped potatoes and skewered sausages from hand to hand. Somewhere else, beyond the fire-light, there was the clink of glass against glass as tall bottles of Guinness were opened and shared amongst the men.

The children's eyes flicked from the flames to the figure of their sister, standing close to the fire talking to Father Duggan's housekeeper. They watched her in silence, any enthusiasm for the festivities around them lost to the knowledge that she would be gone from them tomorrow. Caitriona and Elaine looked forward to moving into her bigger bedroom, but the edge of that excitement was dulled by the prospect of losing their sister. From time to time an aunt or uncle came up to them and squatted down to shake the boys' hands and ruffle the girls' hair, asking if they were looking forward to going back to school in a week's time. The children scowled and shied away, gazing at the patterns in the sand beneath them.

Helen moved amongst her friends and relatives like a ghost. Her eyes searched the shadows for those to whom she had not yet spoken. She listened out for familiar voices rising and falling in the night air, matching names and faces to the sounds.

Then Mattie McHale's voice struck out alone from the crowd as he began to sing. One of the Conneely brothers produced a tin whistle from his jacket and accompanied him. The lilt of other voices ebbed as people fell silent and listened.

> O'Driscoll drove with a song
> The wild duck and the drake
> From the tall and tufted reeds
> Of the drear Hart Lake.
>
> And he saw how the reeds grew dark
> With the coming of night-tide,
> And dreamed of the long dim hair
> Of Bridget his bride.
>
> He heard while he sang and dreamed
> A piper piping away,
> And never was piping so sad,
> And never was piping so gay.

Mattie's voice rose into the clear, salt-scoured air like smoke. The thin notes from the tin whistle amplified the thick stillness beyond the circle of men and women gathered around the flames.

Jarlath heard those first distant notes of Mattie's song. They swarmed through the open windows of his house. He tried to block their sound but found he could not. And still he did not move. He sat alone in the empty, unforgiving house until it began to grow upon him like something unnatural.

Finally, when he could stand it no more, he came to join them, standing away from the crowd.

Mattie continued to sing, his whole body trembling and thrusting with the effort of song.

> But Bridget drew him by the sleeve
> Away from the merry bands,
> To old men playing at cards
> With a twinkling of ancient hands.

> The bread and the wine had a doom,
> For these were the host of the air;
> He sat and played in a dream
> Of her long dim hair.

Whenever Mattie paused to catch his breath the sound of the sea pushed in amongst them, the inexhaustible crease of waves upon the sand filling the air. The sound reassured them; it was the rhythm of their days.

The men heard its sound and were reminded that come morning, when the drinking and singing were done with and the fire had died, they would set out upon its changing waters. The women heard the sound and remembered those great and sudden storms when hours were spent upon the harbour wall scanning the waves for any sign of the return of their husbands and sons.

Helen heard the sound and knew that she would not hear it again until she returned from London. She looked behind her to catch the white break of water against the beach and she thought then of Jarlath. He would know nothing but the sound of that sea, would love nothing but this shore, this land, that had no place for her. She knew that she had loved him in her own way once, had seen so much through his eyes, and had come to understand that it was not enough.

Mattie turned aside to address his own mother with the final verses of his song, and as he did so Helen noticed Jarlath withdrawing into the shadows. Their eyes met and what he saw there was not the distance the past week had put between them, but a longing he had not seen in her before. He looked at her, at the imperfect line of her nose, her eyes holding his. She rose and came towards him, circling the light of the fire and the people gathered in its grasp.

'You came then,' she said when she reached him.

'You will be gone from me tomorrow and I wanted to see you before you go. I couldn't stand it alone in the house any longer.'

They stood apart, almost motionless, the tension imprisoning them in each small movement. Eventually Helen took hold of his forearm and looked into his face as she spoke.

'I'd have had to leave eventually, you must have known that much. There's little to keep me here. A lot of things have changed.'

'I think that we must all know everything,' he said quietly. 'It's just a matter of how much of that knowledge we will admit to ourselves. Yes, I knew you would leave some time – it was in you all along, but I didn't want to see it.'

The notes from the tin whistle rose high in the air as Mattie began the final two verses of his song.

> O'Driscoll scattered the cards
> And out of his dream he awoke:
> Old men and young men and young girls
> Were gone like a drifting smoke;
>
> But he heard high up in the air
> A piper piping away,
> And never was piping so sad,
> Never was piping so gay.

Mattie drew his sleeve across his mouth and blushed when he had finished. A few of the men called out to him from the shadows: 'Good man, Mattie! The Miami will be looking for you any day now!' and, 'You have the voice of a saint, Mattie. If only you'd give up the whiskey the Pope

would canonise you!' The other men and women laughed
and some of the children clapped.

The women began to gather the children, ushering them
away from the last of the bonfire. Gradually the crowd
broke and peeled away. Many of them came to Helen to
kiss her cheek and wish her the best in London. She told
them that she would write soon to tell them of her life
there, and that she would be home for Christmas if the
hospital roster allowed it.

When they were gone Helen leaned in closer to Jarlath
and held him while she waited for the other voices to die
and the air to be still once again. She looked back towards
the land; the houses with their windows lit like lanterns
suspended against the blackness of the hill. She felt the soft
sea-air sliding across her skin and hair and for a moment
she wanted to fix herself in that one point and never leave.
Jarlath held her even tighter and she drew his smell into
her. His hands pressed upon her back and she felt his body
move against her chest.

She heard then the break of water upon the beach,
washing the sand again and again, seeming to wipe away in
one moment all that had gone before and leave the world
anew.

'What will be different here when I am gone?' she asked.

'Everything,' Jarlath whispered. 'Everything will be different for us all from now on.'

After a few more moments she drew him along the beach
towards the stile that led on to the common land. He

helped her over. Helen led the way, her arm stretched behind her to clasp his hand. From time to time she looked back at him, her face pale in the darkness. He could hardly begin to think of what was about to happen to him, to them, and yet he was conscious of a change in her now.

At the copse of trees she paused and turned to him. 'Jarlath,' she said. 'There will only be this once.'

She did not wait for any reply but pushed through the spare trees and down into the hollow they enclosed. Although the darkness was more solid here, bands of moonlight raked through the hollow, picking out her eyes, her teeth, her skin.

She reached for him and found his lips, pushing her body against his until she felt the heat of him destroying her own space.

'Wait,' she said, lifting his hands from her waist. She drew away from him and sat down in the soft grass. Her fingers worked at the buttons of her dress until the gap reached to her navel. Her breasts gleamed in a blade of moonlight when she bent forward to draw the hem of her skirt up to her waist. Discarding his own clothes he moved towards her, his hands reaching for her skin as once again their lips met. Desire and passion now brought them together; and yet, at that moment when their bodies entwined and joined, the patterns of their lives seemed to unravel faster than any memory could recover them.

Later, he lay next to her, their clothes scattered over them for warmth. He drew his finger along the knuckled length of her spine but she did not respond. She was asleep. He kissed her shoulder and settled back against the grass.

He knew that she was beyond him now. She had been all that he had ever wanted to know, all that he had ever wanted to feel. And now, he thought, they were separate again as they would be forever. She must have known this when she led him here and opened herself to him. She must have known that in offering her whole self to him now she was showing him what would henceforth be denied him. Tomorrow she would be free of him, free with her secret deceit. She had laid out her path away from him with the careful, unflinching purpose of a pilgrim.

His eyes watched the moon above their heads. Thin curls of clouds moved across it. He turned away from its gaze and found himself looking at Helen's face. Her eyes were still shut, her lips partly open, a bead of saliva brimming in the corner of a mouth almost turned into a smile.

He found himself reaching for her, his fingers caressing her throat. The breeze moved the trees so that the moon-light cut across her face and as he looked at her she began to re-emerge from sleep. It could not be, he thought in that instant, the face of someone who had set out to deceive him, nor to take anything away from him. It was simply the face of someone who wanted more for herself, more out of her life than could be found there in the fishing village, amidst the small, circumscribed lives she knew too well.

'Jarlath . . .' she mumbled as she woke.

'You've slept,' he said, propping his head upon his hand.

'And I'm still tired. I've a long week ahead of me.'

His fingers traced a line along her collar bone. In his mind's eye the line seemed to run on far and away from him, out into the world.

'Have you been with another man before?' he ventured. 'You seemed to know very well what to do.'

'No, Jarlath.' She sat up all of a sudden, clutching his shirt to her chest. 'No one.'

'I didn't mean anything by it . . . by asking that.' He went to touch her breast, but she turned away from him. His lips found the nape of her neck and he felt her stiffen at his kiss. 'Will you be staying then, after all?' he asked, more in hope than in any certainty.

'Staying?' She turned to him. 'Why should I stay now when what I have wanted all along is to leave?'

'Has tonight not changed things for us?'

'No!' She pulled her dress on over her head. 'I was wrong. I should have seen this coming. I thought that this night together might make it easier for us — that there might be some shared sweetness in my departure, not just this bitterness.'

Her movements as she dressed were uncertain. She did not know where to look, was embarrassed by his nakedness before her. He seized his moment.

'I'll still be here when you are finished in London.'

She flung her shoes at the ground. 'I'll not be back in that case!' She sat down to tie her laces, fingers fumbling with the cord in the darkness. He reached to help.

'Forgive me, please,' she said. 'I meant nothing bad by tonight. I don't want anyone to carry a torch for me while I'm away. I might be back some day, Jarlath, but who knows when? Anyway there's plenty of other girls here will have you.'

'But none like you.' He was clutching at straws now.

She smiled and watched him pull on his trousers, handing him his shirt when he had finished.

It was in the ritualistic elements of their friendship that they now found comfort: the walk back towards their respective homes, the speculation about the weather, the configuration of the stars above their heads, the prospects for the rest of the lobster season. They avoided that which might cause them hurt: the day after, and the days after that, reaching out into the world and eternity like some irretrievable line.

IN THIS WORLD

On the afternoon of the day that she died, Seamus Kelly decided to take one last memento of his beloved wife.

He prepared himself for the task in the bathroom. Standing under the shower, Seamus watched the water flowing across his flaccid, wrinkled skin, as if he could wash away his wife's death, emerge from the bathroom and still find her there on the settee, reading a magazine or doing a crossword. But the stomach cancer had eaten her away from the inside. Like a canker in the apples that were now swelling on the trees in his back garden, it had left her empty and hollow.

When he went to shave (for the second time that day) the blade felt hot and cold at once against his skin, as pure as ice. With trembling hands he had to be careful not to nick his skin. He drew the blade across the shallow stubble at his throat and watched in the mirror as clusters of grey bristles gathered on the edge.

Afterwards, he splashed cold water across his shaven skin, feeling the sting, breathing out noisily. He wet his fingers with lacquer and drew them through his hair, smoothing it back across the bald crown of his head and up behind his ears. Over the years the lacquer had yellowed his hair in places and the bathroom light accentuated this effect. Seamus pulled the suspended cord and the light went out. He stood in the resultant gloom and looked at himself in the mirror. While he dabbed after-shave around his throat he held his own gaze in the glass.

He wanted to think that he had the look of a man who knew exactly what he was doing. In truth, he was unsure of what was going on in his life just then. Now that Anne was gone from this life, nothing was certain.

Anne's corpse lay upon the settee where she had died. Her head rested against an arm-rest, her legs were tucked in underneath her, and her hands were folded across her lap. She looked asleep.

Seamus placed a warm towel on the other arm-rest and went back to the bathroom to get scissors and his shaving equipment. On his way back he took with him a round glass bowl from the kitchen.

He sat down next to her and looked around the room for a few minutes before he could bring himself to look at her properly. When he did, he was mildly surprised to find that she looked almost the same in death as she had in life. Maybe she was a little paler in the cheeks or about the eyes, and it was true, the colour had fled from her lips. But her hair was perfect, not a strand out of place. It was a bouquet of silver light upon her head.

Seamus thought for a moment before gripping his wife by the shoulders and turning her around. Her body was so light and insubstantial in his hands that he could scarcely believe that two hours beforehand she had clutched his wrist with astonishing strength and uttered her final words to him. He laid her gently across his lap, so that her head hung back over his thigh.

His fingers searched through her hair for her scalp, which was cold and hard. Now that he had the measure of her hair he could begin to cut. As he closed the scissors upon the first strands he felt each one yielding to the blades. He cut slowly, almost unsure of his own actions. Ignoring the hairs that fell away from her head, he continued to cut, moving his hand along her scalp so that the scissors could never touch her cold skin.

As he cut through his wife's hair his head was bent down over her face so that he could more closely observe the actions of the scissors' blades. He looked like a jeweller examining the workings of a very small timepiece. He was so close that he could hear the soft crunch as the hairs were shorn in two. Once cut, the hairs fell away from her head with delicate ease; as if, in cutting them, Seamus had spared them the permanence of her death. They drifted slowly, soundlessly, across the backs of his hands and down on to the settee. Seamus concentrated on the cutting and on the drifting hairs, not once allowing his eyes or his thoughts to wander towards Anne's still, silent face.

From time to time Seamus rested the scissors and lifted his eyes from his task. It took a couple of seconds for his eyes to re-focus on the room around him. After a dull,

overcast morning, the sun had come out from behind the
clouds and now spokes of light fanned through the living-
room. The grandfather clock that stood in the alcove next
to the fireplace marked time with a mahogany-muffled
tick-tock. The old furniture was dark and heavy, imparting
an air of permanence and solidity to the room. Seamus
glanced with pride at the rows of books ranged along a
large bookcase: gardening encyclopedias, part-work bind-
ers, Victorian editions on herb gardens, bound volumes of
Amateur Gardener, seed catalogues from before the War.
The symmetry of their dark, stately spines and embossed
titles pleased him. It was an impressive collection.

He returned to his task, the steel scissor blades flashing
in the sunlight that had worked across the room. The silver
locks of hair fell more swiftly now. He had got into his
stride and his two hands moved as one.

After another fifteen minutes he had finished with the
scissors. He turned Anne's head around in his lap to check
for anywhere that he might have missed. Just as her face
was about to turn up towards his, he closed his eyes. With
his hands he felt the features of her face. His fingers kept
finding her nostrils, his thumb burst through her lips and
into her cold, wet mouth. When he could feel that her face
was turned away again he opened his eyes. A queasiness
that had appeared in the pit of his stomach departed. He
satisfied himself that he had removed all of her hair.

As he dropped her shorn hair into the glass bowl he
noticed how the strands fell with the delicate grace of

snowfall, tumbling through the air, buoyed by light. They filled the bowl.

After he had filled a basin with warm water Seamus took a razor to Anne's scalp. He worked a glob of shaving-cream into a lather in the palm of his hand and spread it across her temples. Placing a flattened hand across her face he began to work the razor blade towards the crown of her head. Her soft hair gave way easily, leaving behind an expanse of skin as smooth as glass. The scalp was thin. It did not disguise the mesh of fine blue veins that spread out between her skull and its skin, like a baby's caul. It was a joy to work like this, he thought, to render her head as smooth and perfect as a new-born child's: as if she were being re-born, as if he was bringing her back to life.

Flowers out of season, he thought. The flowers in the wreaths that rested on Anne's coffin were out of season. Carnations, gladioli, astilbe, iris, dwarf phlox.

Seamus examined the wreaths out of the corner of his eye as the priest talked about faith and hope. They were probably imported flowers, forced on beneath polythene, blossoming all year round. It was all he could do not to walk over and examine the arrangements more closely. When he looked up at the altar again he caught the priest's eye. He nodded quickly, nervously, signalling agreement with whatever it was that he had not heard the priest say.

The smell of incense was heavy in the air as he sat in the top pew, thinking about the progress of horticulture. It was only when Roisin, his eldest daughter, tugged at his sleeve that he realised he was supposed to be standing with the rest of the congregation for the Profession of Faith. Never mind, he thought, they will put it down to grief.

After the Mass was over, Seamus went to stand next to the coffin and greet the relatives and friends who had attended. Roisin cried quietly at his side as people shook hands with him and kissed her on the cheek. 'I'm sorry for your trouble,' they invariably said. One neighbour invited the family around for tea the following afternoon, but Seamus reminded her that they had a funeral to go to. She stared back at him, the blood draining from her cheeks, her gloved hand going limp in his grip. She shook a little and mouthed some words that Seamus could not interpret. When he next noticed her, making her way towards the back of the church, he saw that a set of rosary beads was wound so tightly between her fingers that the leather of her gloves was pinched.

When everyone else had gone Roisin said that she and her husband would wait for him in the car outside. He stood alone next to the coffin, listening for the echoes of her footsteps to fade. Finally the church was silent. Seamus sat down for a few moments in the top pew, gathering his thoughts about his wife. He remembered their last breakfast together, an hour spent in blissful ignorance of the fact that it was to be one of her last. They had discussed with brave optimism how they would set about mulching the herbaceous border at the end of the garden. Anne had proposed removing a few of the lupins to give the hostas more air and light. Seamus argued that the hostas would take over if given that much space. Now he regretted contradicting her, and after thinking about it he realised that she was probably right.

She was silent now, enclosed in her oak box, blind to her garland of forced, imported flowers, out of season.

He let himself into the empty house. He walked along the hall in darkness, not wanting to switch on a light because he felt it would emphasise the emptiness. At least for now the house was filled with night.

Leaving his coat draped over the bannister he felt his way up the stairs to the airing-cupboard. Inside, the immersion heater hummed gently, generating the heat that filled the enclosed space. He switched on the small light at the back of the cupboard. Spread out on the shelves before him were tray upon tray of seedlings: begonias, African marigolds, cineraria, marigolds, antirrhinums. He brushed the tips of his fingers along their single-leaved crowns. A few shoots had not yet shaken off fragments of the potting compost they stood in. On others dark seed shells were caught in the intersection between leaf and stalk. His eyes danced over them and he smiled. They had all come up in the space of the two days since Anne had died. Seamus looked at the seedlings for a little while longer, before his attention turned to something else.

At the rear of the airing-cupboard, covered with a square

of muslin, was the glass bowl filled with Anne's silver hair. Seamus carefully lifted the warm bowl out over the curled heads of the seedlings and clutched it against his stomach with one hand while he closed the airing-cupboard door with the other. He stood for a moment feeling the warmth of the bowl pressing in through his clothes and spreading along his skin. Then he walked carefully back the way he had come, the floorboards creaking louder than ever as he descended the stairs in silence.

It was a warm night, thick with noise. Moths beating against an outdoor lamp, a pair of hedgehogs brushing about beneath the garden hedge, the faint hiss of traffic along the roads. Seamus stood at the door to the greenhouse and listened. The glass bowl he held in his hands had cooled by now and he was anxious to get it into the warmth of the greenhouse. The door screeched along its aluminium runners as he pulled it back. He stepped inside and closed the door after him to keep in the heat.

Again he listened. Sometimes Seamus thought he could hear them living and growing, going about their mute business. He thought he could hear their roots sifting through the soil, searching out minerals and moisture. He thought he could hear their leaves unfurl and stretch out into the receptive light and heat of the greenhouse. Sometimes Seamus thought he could hear his plants bursting with life.

He set the glass bowl down on the wooden potting-bench nearest to the paraffin heater and lit the old storm lantern that dangled from the apex of the roof. It flushed the greenhouse with a soft yellowish light. A crane-fly danced up from a darkened corner and bobbed around the lantern. Seamus swiped at it with his hand, then let it be.

Once he had examined the fuchsia and rose cuttings Seamus turned back to the glass bowl. He carefully lifted the muslin and dropped it to the floor. The bowl of silver hair seemed to drain all the available light from the air around it, emphasising its own brilliance. Seamus stared at it for a minute or so, mesmerised. He plunged his hand into the bowl, and watched the strands glowing against his mottled skin.

On the periphery of his field of vision he could just make out the form of his own reflection in the glass wall of the greenhouse. He did not look further, afraid that what he would see there would be a sentimental old man, dipping his hand into a bowl of cut hair. That truth would dispel the magic, would choke the imagination.

He prepared the growing-bag by working some bone meal through the soil. The acrid smell clung to his fingers and he rinsed his hands under the watering-hose. Next he sprinkled the soil with a solution of tomato fertiliser. After wiping his hands on his trousers Seamus lifted a bunch of Anne's hair from the bowl and pushed it carefully into the growing-bag. He stood back from his work once all the hair had been transferred from the bowl to the growing-bag. Anne's hair completely filled the space cut for it in the top of the bag and a few strands hung limply over the edge.

Seamus was pleased with his work and allowed himself a smile. He picked up the glass bowl and stood in the middle of the greenhouse for a few minutes, listening out for the sounds of his plants; disparate whispers in the dark.

Finally, he withdrew. He left the light on. Anne had always slept better once she knew that there was a light on somewhere.

Roisin's grip was vice-like. Her fingers pressed hard into Seamus's wrist as they stood watching the coffin being lowered into the ground. His son, Thomas, stood alone at the other end of the grave, his eyes fixed on the brass name-plate screwed into the coffin-lid. There had been a distance between father and son for many years now, and the length of a grave was the closest they would ever come to each other. Seamus's younger daughter, Susan, was somewhere behind him, leaning upon her fiance's arm. He could just about hear her quiet weeping as they listened to the grating of the straps along the edge of the grave.

Thomas was the first to turn away, walking back towards his car. Seamus watched him leave.

'I'm going after him,' said Roisin, and she followed her brother out of the graveyard. She caught up with him just as he reached the car.

Seamus watched them talking, their elbows propped up on the roof of the car. He looked away when Thomas glanced back in his direction. For a minute or two he watched a border collie making its way across an adjacent tilled field. When he next looked back Thomas was turning his car around and Roisin was making her way back, a white handkerchief held to her nose.

'Aren't the flowers just beautiful,' she remarked when she reached him. 'People are so kind.'

'They'll wither fast,' he thought to himself, 'they've been forced.'

Sleep was something that had to be chased, hunted down by his conscious. He lay still in the centre of the double bed, shutting his eyes against the darkness, waiting for sleep to overtake him. Although his eyes were shut his mind looked out, beyond himself, beyond the darkness that he could feel settling against his heart. He would never look in. Instead, he thought of those things he had neglected during the four days since Anne's death: potting the hyacinths in time for Christmas, the final top-dressing on the lawn, taking out the lupins, staking the freesia at the front-gate. He could think of other things too, but to do so would have kept him awake all night. He needed to sleep.

The sound of whispering woke him a few hours later. He sat up in the bed very suddenly, as if he thought he didn't belong there. In the gloom he could just see the outline of the familiar bedroom furniture. The sound drifted away for a few seconds, then returned. He did not want to hear it. He tried to imagine other noises going on in the house – intruders making their careful way through the rooms beneath him. But he knew there were no intruders here now. None but him.

He knew, too, whose whispering it was, intimately, and went to the window which looked out over the back garden. The greenhouse threw out a penumbra of soft, waxen light, which made the structure appear to float free of the ground. When he opened the window and leaned out the whispering was no louder than before. The sound was that of indistinct syllables borne along on the night wind. Beyond interpretation, they filled the air around him. The night vibrated with their noise.

Seamus leaned back into the room, trying to locate the source of the whispering. One moment he thought that it came from beneath the bed, the next from the wardrobe. Out in the hallway the whispering continued, accompanying him down the stairs, and out, faster now, towards the back garden.

By the time he had reached the middle of the patio the syllables had begun to throb inside his ears, blocking out anything else. He realised that his senses were suffocating.

'Anne!'

He took his hands from his temples and stared around him. Although the retort of his shout still hung in the air, the garden was still and silent, the glow from the greenhouse as constant as ever. The whispering had stopped. But his heart raced and he took a couple of deep breaths to steady himself.

He approached the greenhouse cautiously. Condensation

on the inside of the glass blurred the detail of what lay inside but he could easily see the patch of silver where the growing-bag lay prone on the potting bench.

Inside, the heat was intense and he used a trowel to jam the door wide open. The tomato plants leaned, sweating, against the far wall of the greenhouse. He sprayed them with cold water, examining their broods of small, green fruits as he went from plant to plant. It was inevitable that his attention would finally turn to the hair; his wife's hair. Attending to the other plants was simply a means of stalling, of putting off the moment.

He stared, startled, at the hair. At the point where it had been pushed into the ground, Anne's silver hair had darkened, ever so slightly. He ran his hands across the top of the hair and was surprised to discover that it had not dried out, as he had expected it to. Instead it was soft and supple. Suddenly, he drew back from it, at once curious and afraid. He remembered Anne's bald head, speckled with shaving cream, the net of tiny veins beneath her scalp filled with still blood. He remembered cradling her head in his lap, the feel of her cold skin beneath his fingers, and her wet mouth around his intruding thumb. And then there were her last words.

He kicked the trowel from the doorway and stepped out on to the lawn. The door slid shut behind him and when he looked around all that he really noticed were the fragile shadows cast by the crane-fly as it whirled around the storm lantern.

In the bedroom he closed the window and pulled the

curtains to. He stepped out of his slippers and lay on his back on the bed, his eyes fixed on nothing. After a few moments he closed his eyes and wondered if it was possible to close his ears. He lay perfectly still and breathed in and out, as if waiting for something to happen, for someone to arrive. All that arrived was the memory of her words. He could not keep them away any longer.

'Never again,' she had said, looking into his face. 'Never again.'

There was no breath in the room now but his own. He lay still for a long time, trying not to cry for his dead wife, waiting to fall asleep.

Life resumed in the morning. After breakfast he worked in the front garden, tidying the borders, pinning back the cotoneaster that ran along the pebble-dashed front wall. In neighbouring gardens lawn-mowers growled into life. Mothers walked past his gate, bringing small children to nursery school. A man approached him, asking if he had any blades that needed sharpening. He displayed the stump of a thumb, shorn at the knuckle. Even after Seamus had declined the offer of his services, the man stood around hoping to be asked in for a cup of tea. Eventually he said goodbye and went off up the road.

Roisin called around at lunchtime and made him a cold meat salad. She asked him how he was keeping, and offered to stay with him for the week if it would make life any easier for him.

'No thanks, Roisin' he said. 'Your own family needs you now. I'm fine here at the moment. There's plenty that needs doing in the garden at this time of the year.'

After lunch she wept a little while she sat at the kitchen table, pulling on a cigarette, staring out of the window at the road she had grown up on. Seamus watched her in silence, embarrassed at the sight of her tears. He thought of her as a small child, pigtails bunched together with red elastic, circling around the driveway on a tricycle. She stubbed the cigarette out and stood up.

'Must go,' she said, straightening her skirt.

He saw her to the door and afterwards returned to her seat in the kitchen and looked out of the window as she had done, but he could not cry.

The afternoon passed in silence. There were no more callers, nothing to interrupt the slow rolling away of the hours. After dinner, which he could only half eat, he sat in front of the television watching a chat-show. Bored with that he switched it off and took down a copy of *The Gardening Year* and turned to September. He read for a while but found it difficult to concentrate on anything.

Memories of Anne were beginning to crowd in upon him. He tried to force them from his mind. He saw her in everything around him; in every ornament on the mantel-piece, in every painting hung on the walls, in the very arrangement of the furniture.

A whole family had passed through these rooms, had

flitted around the house like crane-flies. Their sounds had filled the rooms. The walls bore their marks. It was hard to believe that he was the only one left.

Never again. This must have been what she had meant with those words: she would not wish to live her life again. Never again. And yet he had planted her hair in a growing-bag, in the faint, insane hope that it might grow again.

He went out to the greenhouse and stood at the door looking in. Everything was as he had left it the night before. Apart from the trowel, all of the gardening tools were in their place. He pulled back the door. It was distinctly cold inside. He lit the paraffin heater and it jumped into life with a bloom of blue flame. The paraffin fumes began to fill the air and he coughed from time to time.

The cold had not affected her hair. Now, as he looked at the hairs, he realised only too well what had happened, how he had been drawn in by his own dreams. It was capillary action that had caused water to be drawn into the fibres of his wife's hair. It was this that had made them darken. It was this simple, mechanical process that had kept alive his dream of having Anne return to him. He plucked at some of the hairs. They came away easily in his hand and he let them drift to the ground around his feet.

He noticed the crane-fly struggling on the floor of the greenhouse. Its thorax had snapped. He stamped it out of its misery.

Everything had come to an end, as he knew it would.

Now he would have to confront Anne's death and a life lived alone. The selfish idea of going to live with Roisin's family entered his mind, but he dismissed it. That was only an escape, and you could never escape from yourself.

The paraffin fumes were beginning to make him feel dizzy now. He leaned back against a potting-bench. His body seemed to float free of his bones for a moment. He knew that he should winch open the vents or pull back the door, but he didn't have the energy. Anyway, he would be leaving soon.

When he bent to switch off the heater he noticed that the cover of the fuel tank had come off. He took down the storm lantern and used its light to search amongst the potting-trays and propagators for the cover.

As he slipped he knew almost immediately what was about to happen, but was powerless to stop it. The storm lantern broke open, spilling paraffin along the floor. It erupted into flames just as Seamus managed to stand up and reach for the door. The orange flames spread along the potting-bench and stretched up towards the roof. The noise was deafening. Seamus watched the plastic growing-bag melt and the potting compost inside fall to the ground. Anne's hair disappeared within seconds.

He did not want to leave. He could feel his hair scorching and knew that it would soon catch fire. He watched his jacket blackening and then a spark-edged hole appeared on his sleeve. He felt nothing and wondered why he could still breathe. He was tired and knelt down on the hard floor.

The flames poured through the air above his head. There was a fierce shattering sound as the glass panes broke free of their frames.

He knew that his life was over, and that Anne was closer now than ever before. He felt her presence around him, in the air, in that earth, in this world.

DREAM OF FLYING

ALL MORNING AND AFTERNOON he has sat in the front room. We watch him from where we sit and eat lunch upon our knees, not daring to take our customary places at the table in that front room which his indomitable presence has claimed for its own.

He will not take off his coat, nor let go of the black ash walking-stick which he holds out to one side of the armchair. The hand which rests upon the stick is as knobbed and gnarled as the dark ash, its whiskey skin mottled with large freckles that seem to have spread in response to age or gravity. His head pokes out above a soiled shirt collar, a pair of small rheumy eyes seeming to float somewhere between his nose and the flat rim of his cap. Over the years his once taut cheeks have fallen towards his chin, giving him the lazy countenance of a basset-hound.

I cannot remember a single day in the past six years that he has not worn the grey-brown three-piece suit we bought him on his seventy-fifth birthday. Two newer suits hang in his small wardrobe but he has always been too stubborn to even try them on. His charcoal raincoat is frayed at the seams, the lining hangs in threads around the hem, but he is rarely seen without it, summer or winter.

His shoes though, are perfect. Each spring he takes the bus into the city centre and buys a pair of tan brogues from a cobbler on Eustace Street, and each morning we hear him polishing the thick leather as we wake.

Sometimes the twins venture to the doorway between this room and his, standing there for a minute or so, looking at their grand-uncle, waiting for his face to turn towards theirs, for his toothless smile to set them giggling. But this time his face does not turn and they come back to us in silence, disappointment scrawled across their four-year-old faces. He seems caught in a separate existence, as if the strength of his presence in that room has failed to repel the spirits of his past which are locked into a time and a life that cannot now be changed.

Every so often I slam the paper down upon the coffee-table at my feet and look through the doorway at him, vainly hoping that he has noticed my indignation. I fold and re-fold the newspaper to reiterate my point but his expression has not changed for hours on end, and it will not change now.

My wife's freezing-blue eyes gaze out through the rooms. The neutral expression in which those eyes are set betrays the fact that her thoughts are of anywhere but here. His seeming disregard for everyone and everything around him has made her as restless as I am. She snaps at the twins when they come to her, their pleading faces resting momentarily upon her knees.

'Do something about him, now!' she says as she leads them upstairs to their bedroom.

As I listen to her moving about in the room above me I know that I am too afraid of him to do anything. I recall, as she cannot, the countless childhood times when I and my recalcitrant siblings felt the keen edge of his tongue. Although I am that much older now and in many ways he has been absolved of his earlier authority, I know that he still possesses that same innate capacity for the perfect, destructive word, the crippling phrase. Now, I wish that in the descending evening gloom he could be somehow stirred into reprimanding us for our inability to motivate him, to rescue him from his own inertia. But he and I both know that that would be playing into our hands, and he will have no part in any of it.

Anne comes back into the room, snapping a tea-cloth between her hands. She looks first at me and then at the figure in the front room. 'You're still there, so?' she asks aloud, the cloth snapping against the sound of the last word.

She waits, but there is no answer. In his silence he has her beaten. The tension rises and she begins to snap the cloth again and again as she stands in the doorway. Her lips are pursed, blushes of pink showing on the cheeks below those blue eyes.

I feel his spirit begin to rise from the chair and circle the room in opposition to hers.

'Leave him be, Anne. Leave him be.' I stand up and wipe my damp palms upon my trousers.

'I'll not leave him be if he's going to take that sort of attitude in this house.'

I reach for her forearm, noticing the tension there beneath her skin. 'He's tired, let him rest. You'll be his age some day.'

She shakes me off, but I can see that she has softened.

His spirit seems to settle now, as if a great weight has been taken off the room. But still he does not stir.

Later, I go in to him and switch on the lights. He flinches and his head seems to sink even deeper into his layers of clothing, the shiny front of his waistcoat folding and buckling. He tightens his grip upon the walking-stick when I reach across him towards the table lamp at his side. Hurling commentary dogged by interference bleeds from the transistor radio in his lap. It is barely audible and for a moment I wonder whether he can hear anything of it.

'Why won't you speak to us, Michael?' I draw away as I speak.

Although he remains silent I catch a flicker of recognition in his countenance, a slight drawing down of the barrier.

Now that I have made the first incision I will have to give him time. At the front window I watch the lights of the cars as they slow to take the sharp bend in the road upon which our house stands. Behind me I can hear him shifting his position in the armchair, his head turning to look at me, the stick knocking against the wooden arm-rest, his breath quickening for some moments before set-tling again.

'The twins can't wait to be getting out to school next week,' I venture. 'They're cock-a-hoop about the whole thing.'

He does not answer, does not seem interested, but I continue to talk of everyday things: the poor weather, the new Government, the price that the malting com-pany in Athy are paying for barley this season. Every so often I pause and glance back at him, hoping that he will respond. But his head is bent towards the transistor radio. He will not be drawn but I continue with my prattle, knowing that at least it will serve to settle my own growing unease.

No cars pass the house for some time. I seek my reflec-tion in the window but cannot find it, seeing only the room behind me frozen there in the glass before my face. The light that falls through the half-drawn curtain sets down an oblong of dim yellow light upon the lawn out-side. My silhouette stands inside it.

I think of the twins and the adventure they will set out upon in a week's time. It will throw us out of kilter for a while. I know that at first Anne will be relieved to have them out from under her feet, but it won't be long before she begins to miss their presence, their noisy accompaniment to her day's work. What would once have earned them a slap across the back of the legs will then be rewarded with a pat on the back of the head or a kiss on the cheek. She is too soft, she knows, but the school will soon knock the corners off them.

They have spent this past week marching hand in hand around the house with their identical school-bags slung over their shoulders. Even now, as they sleep, the school-bags hang on the corner-posts of their beds. Inside each is a copybook and a pair of orange pencils, each identical and pared to the same degree of sharpness and length so that neither will have any advantage over the other.

I have chosen the school they will attend, but now feel more like an outsider, a casual observer, during their weeks of preparation for school. Each evening I return from the office to find them eating at the kitchen table, the drawing books and marker pens cleared away into a drawer until the next day, school-bags already suspended from their bed-posts. Together we watch the evening news, the three of us crushed on the settee, until it is time for them to be kissed goodnight and put to bed. This has been the pattern for so long now that I accept it almost without thought. And it saddens me to know that in a week's time this daily routine will be no different for me, if all too different for them.

I cannot show it. It is the way things are now. Although my wife's and sons' lives are about to be changed forever it will make little difference to mine. They grow in my shadow now, like the tiny daisies whose closed blossoms bow within the oblong of illuminated grass beyond this window.

I have become increasingly irritable and silent over the past week but will not admit to it. I have begun to live my life in retrospective; recalling the afternoon upon which my sons were conceived (amidst the desperate reparation for a drawn-out argument, rain thrown against the windows), the evening they were born (heady with the scent of forsythia in the hospital grounds), their first unsteady steps across the kitchen floor (each perfectly matching the other's progress). It all seems so close to me now. Hardly any time has passed and yet I have become detached from their lives.

Now, as a new beginning looms for them, I want to stretch out their four brief years, re-involve myself in them so that I might approach this threshold with more understanding and less mourning for that which now seems irretrievable.

I hear him struggle to rise from the armchair, bearing down upon the walking-stick with both hands and almost levering himself into a standing position. I listen intently, not wanting to turn around for fear of distracting him from his purpose. His carefully polished shoes begin to shuffle across the floor, the tapping stick leading the way. There is a pause as he reaches the door and then another sound which at first I do not recognise: the thin rustle of paper. I turn just enough to see him lay a folded letter down upon the writing bureau next to the door. He closes the door after him. The almost unbreathable atmosphere in the room seems to have departed. I lean back against the edge of the windowsill, feeling the tension leak from my body, my eyes fixed upon the bundle of pale blue paper he has left behind.

I fumble it open with unsteady hands, half-afraid that at any moment he might burst in upon me. But I know that it is not in him to do anything without a firm purpose. I spread the crisp, lightweight paper upon the bureau.

> Buzzards Bay
> Massachusetts
> USA

Dear Michael,

Have you forgotten us all over here? We would call you but you have never given us Paul and Anne's number and we don't like to ask them for it straight out. So, I'm writing you in the hope that you'll accept the enclosed airline ticket for next week.

You know that we haven't seen or heard from you since poor Annie passed away – is it really twelve years since then? Time passes too quickly nowadays and we've all gotten older than we should.

If you do come over, call me from Logan

Airport and I'll send your nephew Jim to pick you up. Bring along some snaps of the twins – I hear they're real cute. We're all looking forward to seeing you after all this time, and hearing more of those stories you were great for telling in the old days.

love always,
Maura

As I fold the letter out further the airline ticket falls on to the bureau. It is obvious that he has paid it more than just a cursory glance: there are thick smears of red carbon ink where he has thumbed through it. The pitifully short letter has been read over and over again by the same pair of eyes, the fragile paper folded and re-folded so that it is almost split.

He has never left Ireland, never set foot upon any other soil. There are few more rooted in this island than he. His brothers and sisters made their homes in America, Scotland and New Zealand, but he remained behind to tend the small family farm. For years they tried to persuade him to sell the land and start a new life with them, on foreign soil. But he would have none of it. When he finally married on his sixtieth birthday his brothers and sisters said that it was just to show them that now he could never leave. But nine years later his wife was dead and their persuasion grew more intense than ever before. In reply he spent the following summer re-thatching the roof of the farmhouse and pouring a new concrete floor on the milking parlour. Now he would *never* leave.

In the end it was they who returned, reclaimed by the inexorable draw of nostalgia and tradition; some leaving grown families behind them, others bringing everyone back.

I hear him descending the stairs, the stick tapping against the wooden bannisters. I re-fold the letter and put it back where and how I had found it, before taking up my place at the window, seeming to look out for the slowing cars.

As he comes in he holds the door open with his foot and picks up the letter. He makes an issue of pushing it back into a pocket and all the time I feel his eyes upon me. I listen to him cross the room behind me and as he makes to sit down in the armchair, I speak:

'Will you go?'

There is a short pause in his movements as he stops to absorb my question, an exhalation, and then the creaking of the armchair as it takes his familiar weight once again.

'No,' he says softly. 'I won't be going anywhere.'

'Do you have any mind to go at all?'

'No, none.'

I wait in the hope that it will be he who speaks next, but in the end I am forced to break the silence before it settles back upon him and the chance is lost as if forever.

'Do you think, then, that *I* could use the ticket? I'd love to go.'

'You?' he says incredulously. 'You have a job and a family; you can't be going all that way at the drop of a hat.'

'It could be easily arranged with the office. There's nothing to stop me. I could be on the plane tomorrow.'

'It's *my* bloody ticket. If I'm not going, then nobody is going. That's all there is to it.' He starts to tap the walking-stick off the edge of the fireplace, making a dull thud against the tiles. I know that no matter what he might say to me now, he is unsettled.

'Why won't you go, Michael? What's to stop you?'

'You're beginning to sound like my brothers and sisters did. For thirty years that was all I ever heard out of them. And what good did it do any of them? Twelve years now and not a word.' A smile creeps across his lips. 'Not a word out of them,' he breathes. 'All quiet now.'

He leans back into the armchair, letting the stick fall against his knee and rest there. His eyes flick towards the clock upon the mantelpiece and then he settles. He will go up to bed soon, taking with him the folded letter, the ink-smeared airline ticket, the wooden stick polished by skin and cloth.

I undress in the dark. Slowly. Allowing myself to feel the clothes slide from my skin, to feel the cool air press itself against my nakedness. I set the clothes upon a chair and sit at the edge of the bed, my hands feeling the piping that runs the length of the mattress. The elements of the room begin to assume their shapes around me, suspended as they are in the blackness, the boundaries of what had a few minutes ago seemed an infinite darkness.

For a moment or two I listen to the sound of Anne sleeping, imagining those eyes beneath her soft eyelids. And as I listen to her sound, it becomes the pitch of the stillness within this room. I lie back upon the bed, turning on my side and towards the sleep I know will come.

But even now he is tearing at the edge of the stillness. I hear the dead click of the light switch in his bedroom next door. I turn on to my back and raise my head from the pillow, listening out for more. I hear his feet shuffling across the thread-bare carpet, his wardrobe being opened, and the chiming clang of the empty wire hangers along the rail. Then the shuffle back across the floor, even more slowly this time.

I think of the twins learning to walk, their feet moving in tandem across the floor, each step more certain than that which went before. Until eventually they *are* walking, stumbling towards my outstretched arms, their faces a mixture of fear and delight.

Now he makes careless noises as he moves uncertainly about the room. There is the rustle of paper, then the thin slapping sound of cards or photographs being quickly flicked through. Occasionally there is the creak of bed-springs as he sits down to rest awhile. I begin to wonder if these activities of his are a means of allaying the memories that, like a fever, are strongest and most real at night. I wonder too what the letter has roused in him; this unwelcome agitation of his memory, that has for so long waited, unstirred, untouched.

I listen to his movements until Anne turns in her sleep, pressing her head against my neck, her arm reaching across me, our bodies folding together. Against my back I feel her heart moving beneath skin and bone, and as I close my eyes and fall into sleep that rhythm of nerve and muscle becomes another sound: the beating of wings, the dream of flying.

In the morning I find his door ajar, the bed made, his wardrobe empty save for the wire hangers. The windows are wide open, the curtains sucked outwards by the breeze that has already scrubbed the room of his smell. It is as if he has never been there.

I dress quickly and go out to the car. The cold strikes me as I sit in behind the steering-wheel. Summer is almost at an end. For a moment I wonder if I should just leave him be, but eventually I swing the car out on to the bend in the road.

He has not gone far when I find him; trudging towards the railway station, a small suitcase in one hand, the walking-stick in the other, the same old clothes. I stop the car some yards ahead and watch him approach. His expression never changes, not even when I open the door and he sits into the passenger seat. He straightens his cap, rests his folded arms upon the suitcase, and looks out at the road ahead of us. He jolts a little as the car takes off, and then he is still, his eyes on the road, a finger tapping against the edge of the suitcase. Ahead of us the road curves away into the distance and out of sight.

I know that this is not an easy journey for him. It is more than a journey. It is the shedding of the skin of defiance he has worn for almost a lifetime. It is the giving in to something he has kept at bay for years and which he has neither the strength nor the will to avoid any longer.

'Why the sudden change of mind, Michael?'

He starts when I speak, and the finger ceases its tapping. He shifts in the car seat. His eyes flicker around the landscape that rushes towards us within the frame of the windscreen. I sense that inside his head he is replaying those incidents and moments when life seemed to turn one way or another, sometimes changing everything, but more often than not, changing nothing.

'I had dreams last night,' he says in a voice that is unusually thin, as if it might fail at any moment. 'I had dreams of flying back to visit my brothers and sisters.' He seems almost apologetic. 'But, of course, they're not there any more – gone.' He breathes out deeply, as if releasing a half-century's regret. 'And, you know,' he continues, 'when I was a younger man I used to dream that by staying here, in this country, I could outshine them all, turn water into wine, or what have you.'

'So, why the journey *now*?'

'I'll not rest until I've seen what they all saw.' He thumps me solidly on the shoulder, and grins. 'Sure, maybe I will get more out of it than they ever did. Maybe I'll make something of it.'

GIVING GROUND

SISTER MICHAEL, her eyes still clotted with sleep, ran cold water into the sink. As she bent to wash she noticed again the bare plaster wall, its surface indelibly stained with the inseparable splashes of countless washings. And at that moment when the cold water upon her face caused her to pass into wakefulness, those innumerable stains seemed to her to be the measure of her days in the house around her.

After she had washed she went downstairs. Her footsteps echoed in the hallway as she passed along it towards the front door. She was aware of her own sound amidst the stillness of early morning. Each noise she made filled the air, amplified the silence.

Sister Michael swung the door open and looked to see if anything had been left for her overnight. Three small, foil-wrapped packages leaned against the door-frame. She picked them up and stacked them in the crook of her arm, then turned back into the silent house.

In the scullery she stripped the foil from the first parcel and tested the freshness of the wholemeal bread inside. After she placed the bread into a wicker basket she brushed the crumbs from her black habit, watching them bounce soundlessly on the linoleum floor.

She passed into the front room and knelt down in the middle of the wooden floor facing the picture of the Sacred Heart. Putting her palms together she began to pray, each verse of adoration coming to her without effort, almost without thought. Now she was as still as the sleeping house around her.

Above her head fragile spokes of sunlight found their way across the white ceiling. Motes of dust wheeled in the light. She craned her neck to watch.

Squeezing her palms even closer together she imagined her heart beating inside her like the eternal flame at the still centre of a church, its doors wide open, flooded with the light of God. This was the church she had built with her own faith, prayer by breathed prayer, blessing by blessing.

Sister Michael kneeled and prayed for almost three-quarters of an hour until she heard the familiar sound from one of the upstairs rooms. She blessed herself before touching her lips to the frame of the picture depicting the Sacred Heart. And as she kissed the saliva-stained wood she heard the other tiny voices start up in the rooms above her. She went up to them.

A brass crucifix was fixed to the centre of each of the three doors that led off the upstairs landing. As she pushed open the first of them the crying seemed to intensify in the other two rooms, so that she paused before pushing the door wide open.

The room was small, with a narrow, curtained window at the opposite end. Behind the door was a low chest of drawers, filled with towels, cloths and small, square nappies. Next to this was a wooden kitchen chair. On either side of the room stood a pair of identical white wooden cots.

Sister Michael went to the first cot and looked down upon its crying occupant. The child's red, wet face looked back at her, its tiny hands crunched together beneath its chin. She watched the child moving its tongue along its smooth pink gums as it cried. She reached down for it and picked it up, pressing its trembling body against her chest and shoulder. She rubbed the baby's back and it soon ceased crying. Its eyes seemed to wobble in their sockets as it attempted to fix its stare upon the floor. She walked to the window and drew back the curtains, letting the light of winter through the netting that had stuck to the condensation upon the glass. Later, she would open the window and allow the cold air to scour the room clean of its soured nightsoil smell, but for now the children needed to be fed. As she gazed at the marbled vision of the outside world caught now in the window pane, she began to feel the baby's heartbeat seeping through her habit.

After she had pulled back the curtains in all three bedrooms and soothed the six children, Sister Michael set their bottles to warm in a large pan of water on the range in the kitchen at the rear of the house. While the bottles warmed she dragged out the shallow steel sheep trough from its resting-place behind the door. This she half-filled with cold water. When the bottles were warm enough she would boil the water in the pan and add it to the contents of the trough. She laid out a pair of thick towels upon the cold stone floor before taking the warm bottles upstairs.

Sister Michael sat on the wooden chair and rested the first baby in the crook of her elbow. It sucked on the teat of the bottle and she felt its eager hunger pressing against her own chest. Dribbles of watered milk made their way along the child's cheeks and sank into her apron. She watched the bubbles bloating inside the glass bottle and absent-mindedly swung the door to and fro with her foot.

While the baby fed, she thought of the babies' unknown mothers, ignorant now of their children's nameless fates. No one had ever come to the house to reclaim a child; she had never had word from her Mother Superior that any had been returned to its own mother. Once or twice she had seen young women, some merely teenagers, standing at the front gate looking in upon the house. She could feel their eyes following her movements about the rooms, but she had always been careful to shield the children from the gaze of the outside world.

It was then that she felt the child's fingers fasten upon her own. She stared down at its hand, the unwarranted contact surprising her. Sensing something, the child stopped feeding and turned its eyes towards her face, its pupils dilating, blackening. Its grip tightened and she twisted her hand to free her finger. When the child attempted to grab on to something else it found only the empty air.

Feeling uneasy, Sister Michael encouraged the child to

feed again, pushing the teat back between its milk-laden lips. She could feel herself flushing, becoming acutely aware of every element in the room around her: the gauzed frame of light tumbling through the window and across the floor, the listless snore of the other child in its cot, the throb of life running through the child in her lap. There seemed to be a great, palpable strangeness in things. Strange that she, a woman, should feed this helpless, unknowing child and still recoil from its too-intimate touch. Strange that in tending these nameless, unbaptised children, these spoils of evil, she should be working towards the greater glory of God. Strange, she thought, and yet, not strange at all. Each of these children was rich with the promise of the future, with the promise of their own children in years to come; and here was she, crushing her own instinct, recoiling from theirs, so that they might one day live according to their impulses. Her promise of the future still echoed (but fading now in her middle years) in her womb, dismantled every month. This, she could not deny. But what had been compromised for so long? Faith or fertility?

The child was asleep in her arms. She laid it back down in the cot and selected another bottle before waking the other baby for its feed. Once the second child had been returned to its cot she went to the window and opened it. The sash cords were too taut and the window shot upwards. The sudden cold air seized the edge of the room, trapping itself against her skin. She gasped at its touch and stood away for a second before pulling the window down once more. Calming, she looked out at the hard winter light spread across the land. A faint miasma of frozen fog clung around a hawthorn copse. A jaundiced sun hung over the tops of the hawthorns and above, the sky was a cracked-ice blue, the colour of bluebells. She looked down at the rectangular vegetable plot at the rear of the house. What few vegetables that lingered there were frozen now, covered in a christening of hoar-frost. She should ask Father O'Hanlon to dig them for her on his next visit, although she felt reluctant to do so – he had done so much for her already.

By the time the last of the six babies had been fed it was almost time to bathe the first of them. She set the pan of water to boil on the range and while the tiny heat bubbles gathered against the metal she soaped and scrubbed the work surfaces.

Some time later she mounted the stairs and lifted the first child from its cot and brought it down to the kitchen for its bath. She undid its nappy and dumped the soiled cloth into a steel pail. The child kicked its legs furiously and bawled but she held the child as steady as could be until it either grew accustomed to the water or tired of protest. Eventually it stilled and she sat the child down in the bottom of the trough, ladling water on to its head with cupped palms.

As she bathed the child, her wet hands moving from limb to limb, her mind drifted and she imagined that in her own way she was baptising the child. She had not the power of that sacrament within her, but in many ways she was inculcating these children into His family. Soon, their new families would bring them to their own parish churches to be christened; but for now they were destitute souls, still stained with original sin.

Baptism formed her earliest memory. Not, of course, her own baptism, but that of her brother, younger than her by two years. She remembered the candles his godparents held as they stood on either side of the priest while he trickled water across her brother's forehead. No matter how hard she tried, she had never been able to expand upon that scene. She remembered no faces, no voices, no words, only the presence of God in the baptismal font, in the unsteady waxen light, in the priest's silken vestments that glistened like her childhood idea of heaven. He was the Father she remembered from those years long ago, and not her natural father, who had died of a heart-attack five years after she had entered the convent. By the time that she had learned of his death, her mother too was dead, lying side by side with her husband in a grave sunk in the sand, looking out on the Atlantic Ocean in Donegal.

She shed the memory as swiftly as she had conjured it up. It was important not to dwell on these mortal things that had occurred outside her relationship with God. Death was as much a part of His mystery as life.

After each child had been washed and had had its nappy changed she poured soda crystals into the pail of soiled nappies and stood it outside the back door. She went out to the garden and began to take down the six squares of cloth that hung frozen upon the washing-line.

The ankle-high grass crunched beneath her feet. Ice-clusters clung to the bottom of her habit. The nappies came away from the line like trembling sheets of ice, and she cracked then folded them upon one another. By this time her hands were almost blue from the cold so she squeezed them together between her knees to help the joints move more easily. The cold was such a hardship. At least in summer she could bring the children outside and lay them down on thick blankets spread upon the soft grass. They slept more easily there than in the stifling confines of their narrow bedrooms.

But it was not in her to wish for any more than she had already got. Besides, she thought, the year passes so quickly. Even the seasons seemed to contract as one year followed another. Hardly were the bulbs up but the leaves were spinning from the trees, circling the house. Hardly had they fallen but the snow would arrive and she would break the ice on the front path only to find the dead leaves encased therein, like the fossil memories of sea shells in ancient rock.

So many children had swept through the house during the accelerating seasons and years that it did not bear thinking about. They had become faceless memories for her now. None stayed long enough for her to see them grow. Only the dead lingered in the catalogue of children that was her memory. Their cold, stiffening tiny forms asleep but not asleep under the covers. Asleep forever, she would like to think, but knew that God had willed their death if not their birth.

A month or two later there would be another child to take its place between those same sheets, curled and curved into that same hollowed mattress, like a sea shell upon its bed of sand.

The following morning the parcel that had been left on the doorstep froze hard to the cold stone so that when Sister Michael went to pick it up she almost fell over. Once she had steadied herself she prised the parcel from the step and kicked away the film of ice, lest Father O'Hanlon slip on it should he call upon her later in the day.

Setting the parcel down upon the wooden kitchen table she undid the string that sealed the thick brown paper. She spread the paper out. Inside was a bag of sugar, two blocks of home-made butter wrapped in muslin, a box of salt and a circular pan of soda bread wrapped in a fresh cloth. She unwrapped the bread and shook the loose flour from the cloth before folding it and laying it aside. She would remember, later, to put the cloth back on the doorstep so that its unknown owner could reclaim it after nightfall.

She returned to the front door and stood there for a while, watching the blackbirds and wrens flitting through the hedge that surrounded the front garden. Whoever had left the parcel that night had left faint footprints in the fur of frost upon the path. They were small footprints. She could never imagine any man making that night-time journey from the village with a food parcel under his coat. But the wives and mothers had made frequent visits at the dead of night, delivering supplies of food, clothes and toiletries on a regular basis. Yet, not one of those women would ever admit to their clandestine mercy missions. Sister Michael knew that in giving to the orphanage these women believed that they were in some strange way atoning for their sins and the sins of the society they lived in. Thus, none would admit to giving, for to admit would be to imply that one had sinned.

She closed the door and went back into the still centre of the house. The fire in the range had sunk low and she pushed more turf in upon the embers. It hissed and spat for a few minutes before the flames truly took hold, and then everything was quiet again. She walked about the downstairs rooms, drawing curtains and opening the windows just enough to admit a draught that would draw any stale air out. The hard winter light spilled into the rooms, splashing across the plain walls, pouring into the corners, shadows staining the floors.

In the front room she knelt again to pray. And as she prayed she sought forgiveness for the sins of the mothers who had borne the children asleep in the upper rooms of the house, for the men who had undoubtedly forced themselves upon those women, and for the villagers, whose countless, unknown sins could never be absolved by the gifts they left upon the doorstep each night.

In her prayers she remembered, not for the first time, her parents and prayed for their souls. Such prayer was forbidden by the Order, but she could not help herself. This contravention of the laws troubled her and she pressed her palms closer together, trying to force thoughts of her family from her mind.

The draught that circled the rooms dragged at her habit, sucking it around her figure. Her knees felt sore upon the hard boards. The natural world pressed in on her as she opened her eyes and looked for the picture of the Sacred Heart upon the wall. The glass had caught the angled sunlight and she saw there nothing but her own image, like a shadow upon quicksilver. Swiftly, she closed her eyes and conjured the church inside her heart, its eternal flame blown one way and then another, clinging to its tentative existence. The doors were beginning to close and she could make out the evanescent figures of her parents and brothers taking their places in the pews at the rear of the church.

It took some time for the first knock upon the door to enter her consciousness and by then there was a second, louder knock. The sound shook her and seemed to reverberate throughout the house. The children did not stir. She quickly blessed herself and got up off her knees. Her heart hurt with some unknown pain as she went to the front door.

'Good morning, Sister!' Father O'Hanlon stood upon the doorstep, his bicycle leaning against the front wall. 'Just a moment,' he said, turning towards the basket on the front of the bicycle.

While his back was turned she put her hands to her cheeks and felt the hot blood that had settled there beneath her skin, like a subcutaneous mask. She smoothed her habit and held her breath, struggling to regain her composure. She exhaled and her breath rose in the freezing air before her face.

Father O'Hanlon turned around again, a sheet-wrapped bundle in his arms, like a swaddled child. Sister Michael stepped aside and allowed him in the door.

'It's a cold morning to be cycling without a coat on, Father,' she said, noticing the silvered web of frozen dew upon his lapels.

'Sure, it's good for the circulation, Sister, and when I get here this house is always grand and warm.'

She looked at him, at his shoulders hunched over the cradled white bundle in his arms. She ushered him into the front room where she had been praying. Everything there seemed normal now. The Sacred Heart looked out at the room from behind the glass. The light had settled. Outside the window the trees were still.

'Here,' she said, stretching her hands towards the bundle in his arms, 'let me take that from you.'

'No, Sister. I'll put it down on a table if I may. We can get a good look at it then.'

She showed him to a small, square table in the cusp of the bay window at the front of the room. The sheet began to fall away as he righted the object and the face of the Madonna appeared. He removed the rest of the sheet and revealed the child Jesus astride the Madonna's hip, its dark, unseeing eyes staring out into the room.

'There now!' Father O'Hanlon exclaimed. 'How's that?'

Sister Michael stood back from the figures and pondered them for a few moments, touching a finger to her lower lip. The Madonna's shawl was furred with dust and the sunlight picked this out so that from one moment to the next the figure seemed to move almost imperceptibly. She turned away. 'It's beautiful, Father O'Hanlon, beautiful.'

'I . . . I got it from another parish. They'd had it under the sink in the sacristy for years before I chanced upon it when I was concelebrating a wedding there the other week.' He flicked at the film of dust, launching small plumes of it into the sun-struck air that flowed about the Madonna and Child.

'Will you have a cup of tea?' she ventured.

'I will,' he replied, not turning around, his attention upon the rediscovered figure.

Father O'Hanlon seemed lost in his own thoughts as he continued to flick dust from the plaster clothes of the Madonna. Sister Michael looked at him, at the old, old black suit that he wore. Over the many years it had taken on a greenish hue, gone shiny from over-pressing at the lapels and cuffs, and had acquired a permanent odour of hair oil and mothballs. The seams had loosened so that the stitching showed and the collar creaked whenever he turned his neck to one side. He still had his bicycle-clips on, and his tan shoes were scuffed about the toes.

'I thought, Sister,' he said, his back still turned in contemplation of the figures, 'I thought that the Madonna and
Child would be very appropriate for this household.' He
turned around, the sunlight bouncing from him, gilding his
grey hair. 'You know, the household you have above you
here.' His eyes flicked momentarily towards the ceiling.
'The Madonna protecting the child, even though it was not
her own, but God's. Don't you see, Sister Michael?'

'Yes, Father,' she replied, her hands gripping together
nervously, each seeking to arrest the movement of the
other. 'But I had never quite considered my station in
God's plan quite like that.' She smiled, squinting against
the light that came around him.

'He moves in ever mysterious ways, Sister Michael.
When I was studying theology in Saint Pat's, I never . . .'

'Father O'Hanlon,' she interrupted, 'while the tea is
drawing you could be changing the light-bulb in the
hallway there. It blew on me last night and I'm afraid I can't
reach it.'

'Yes, yes, of course. I'll do that right away. I'm sure that
you have other things I could be getting on with while I'm
here.'

When the tea had drawn she lifted the teapot from the
range and poured the dark liquid into a white mug. She
splashed some milk in afterwards and stirred in a spoon of
sugar. She could hear the creaking of the footstool as Father
O'Hanlon fumbled with the shade and bulb in the hallway.
Every so often there was a grunt of impatience as one or

other of the components slipped in his hand. She carried the tea and two slices of gingerbread into the front room.

Just as she was setting the tray down upon a table she happened to look up in his direction. The doorway into the hallway held Father O'Hanlon framed within it. His head, however, was out of view above the door. She watched his feet moving about upon the footstool as he sought to fit the bulb. The blown bulb was pushed into his lapel pocket. Feeling something coming over her, she closed her eyes, and in that moment she remembered her own father. She remembered his sound, his presence in the house of her childhood. She opened her eyes but the memory drifted. She shut them again to reclaim it. The half-remembered smell of her father's tobacco seemed to linger somewhere in the room around her. She remembered the sound of his feet upon the wooden stairway, the splashing of water in the bathroom as he rinsed his razor, his voice calling her from her bed for school. No words – they didn't matter now – just the sonorous boom of his voice about the house, tied to everything he was, or had been. Had been, before she had any chance to know who he really was.

When she opened her eyes again Father O'Hanlon was pushing the footstool back into the room. He flicked the light-switch a couple of times to ensure that the bulb was fitted correctly. 'You were deep in prayer for a few moments there, Sister Michael,' he said. 'It does me good to see His strength so alive in you.'

She set the tray hurriedly down on the table and returned to the kitchen. The blood had returned to her face. She felt her heart beating swiftly within her. She went to the sink and ran the cold tap, slowly at first, then faster; louder and louder, water thudding, drumming off the thin reverberating steel. Her hands cooled beneath its flow, the cold jet of water forcing her fingers apart.

Her hands were numb by the time she turned off the tap. Puddles of water lay upon the floor at her feet. Bright beads of it clung to the front of her black habit. There were spatters upon the window. But the memories had gone.

From the front room came the sound of Father O'Hanlon stirring more milk into his tea. She heard the metal spoon scraping the bottom of the mug. She closed her eyes again, this time to pray, her wet hands adhering together, cold water running along her forearm.

At first she could only conjure the familiar vision of the church of her heart, emptied of her family. The eternal flame was steadier now. As she focused upon it she saw a lone figure standing in the doorway, the pure, absolute light of Christ flowing around him; in his arms the Madonna and Child with its dead, staring eyes slowly animating.

Eventually, as the church of the heart dissolved, a few, fractured prayers came to her, bound together by the ticking of the carriage clock upon the dresser at the far end of the room. It was as if the beats of her heart were at one with the beats of the clock, their combined rhythm drawing prayers in and casting them out into that eternal, everlasting lapse of space and time, inhabited by her God.

She opened her eyes and was still looking out of the window when she heard his feet upon the floor behind her. Father O'Hanlon stood in the doorway, the white mug poised delicately between his hands, as if he were about to offer it to her. The light from the front room seemed to surge against his back, profiling him, causing his features to blend with the blackness of his clothing so that only the proffered whiteness of the mug could be distinguished.

'Sister Michael,' he said, stepping forward. 'The garden needs a bit of seeing to.' His eyes strained towards the garden framed in the window behind her. 'I'll see what I can do with it.' He handed her the mug as he went towards the back door. She was almost afraid to receive it.

As the door closed behind him and his feet crunched out across the frozen grass, a child began to cry in the rooms above her. Sister Michael set the white mug down upon the counter and went upstairs, taking the steps as ponderously as she remembered her father had done; as if each footfall provoked a fresh thought, or summoned a different memory.

Father O'Hanlon spent the rest of the morning working in the garden. Sister Michael watched him from the windows as she went about the daily routine of waking and feeding the children. She watched him lift what few parsnips remained, their crowns split with frost, their pale flesh blotted and pocked with rot. Afterwards, he turned the dark soil, drawing the dead-yellow leach-pan up to the surface so that the frost could break it down to a crumb. He seemed to draw everything in that soil to the surface, leaving it exposed, naked, to the elements.

As she watched she remembered her father's broad back bent over his native Donegal soil, the jarring ring as a fork-prong struck the rock that lay so close beneath the surface of their small farm. She could see him now, his arms straining with the weight of a rock as he repaired a dry stone wall. She smelled the sweet musk of fresh clay from his boots where they stood inside the kitchen door. She could see now the steam that rose from his jacket when he left it over the range to dry. His memory was almost real to her.

And when she turned away from the window the faces that stared up from the cots were not just the faces of unknown, nameless children, but those of her younger brothers, her nieces and nephews, who shared her blood and perhaps some vestige of her appearance, and who were lost to her now.

Later, she brought some tea out to Father O'Hanlon. He took the mug in both hands, warming his palms against the crockery, vapour rising to meet his face before he could wet his lips with the hot tea. She stood some feet away from him, cradling her own mug, her eyes fixed on the ground at her feet. Father O'Hanlon looked away, towards the horizon, up at the sky, or back towards the house, like a maritime navigator fixing his position upon an empty sea.

His face had reddened from his labours, the broken veins upon his cheeks and at either side of his nose more prominent now. He did not speak, as though the cold and the effort expended had consumed his speech. When he had finished he wiped his lips with the back of a hand and returned the mug to her. He set back to work, the fork swinging, clay broken again and again and again.

As she made her way back towards the house she looked around her at the fields and the skies that hung over them. The slanted, refracted light was failing. Even the stone walls that hugged the ground cast thick, rectangular shadows upon the grass and newly-broken ground. Everything, she thought, was becoming a part of the shadows. She closed the door and entered the pitch well of the kitchen.

When the light had failed he came in and they ate in the kitchen. Sister Michael delighted in the pleasure of cooking a proper meal for two, instead of the usual single setting upon the table and the small sauce-pots in which she would boil her vegetables. Tonight, a glass bowl was piled high with potatoes, and the chopped carrots and parsnips filled another dish. Father O'Hanlon said grace and while they ate he told her what he would plant in the garden once the days had lengthened and the weather had warmed. She listened intently, nodding from time to time. But what was on her mind, what troubled her most, was the way in which the ordinary, mortal world was pushing its way into her life. And her greatest grief was her inability to control something so natural, so corruptible.

After they had eaten, Father O'Hanlon retired to the front room. With the washing up done Sister Michael went up to tend to the children. Halfway up the stairs she looked down through the bannisters and saw Father O'Hanlon kneeling to pray in the front room. He went down on one knee, resting his elbow and forearm upon the other. He bowed his head and took a set of rosary beads from his pocket and looped them twice around his thumb. As they swung to and fro she was aware of their keeping time with the beat of the clock which she could still hear from the kitchen. Slowly, his whispered prayers filled the dimly-lit room. His shadow moved about the floor as he shifted the weight from his knee to his other foot, mitigating his own discomfort. She went on up the stairs, his prayers seeming to rise with her and follow her into each room.

She went from child to child, ensuring that they were sleeping flat upon their stomachs, straightening their blankets. In each narrow room she stopped to listen to their breathing, her hand resting on the door-handle for a moment before moving on to the next room, and in the space between rooms there came the sound of Father O'Hanlon's prayers.

In her own bedroom, she lingered. She looked out of the window before drawing the curtains. A delicate sheen of frost clung to the inside of the window-glass and her breath rose before her in the unheated bedroom. The lone ceiling bulb seemed impossibly harsh, as if its light increased the cold within the room. She went out, noticing as she paused upon the landing that the prayers from below had ceased.

'Will you have another cup of tea, Father?' she asked as she came through the door. But he could not reply. He was asleep in the armchair, his mouth sagging open, the rosary beads thrown across his lap. His intermittent snores scattered across the room, surprising her while she wiped the table clean.

She could not bring herself to dust the Madonna and Child, adjusting the lamp instead so that its light would not profile the figure. While she tidied away the cups and saucers the dead eyes of the child Jesus seemed to follow her around the room. She escaped the silent stare and went into the kitchen.

She spent an hour or so there, shuffling the jars on the dresser, refilling the salt cellar and the sugar bowl, checking the muslin lids on the preserves. She examined her reflection in the kitchen window, something she very rarely did, so that her appearance was never something immediately familiar to her. There was no mirror in the house, and no need for one. She straightened the line that the edge of her veil made across her forehead and swept a few stray threads from the front of her habit. Reaching behind her with both hands she grasped the thick black gown and pulled it tight against her skin. She turned a little to the side and glanced at her profile before releasing the gown. Then, while the cloth assumed its natural concealing form, she grew suddenly angry at herself for this submission. She had learnt, like all the other sisters had learnt, that what was natural to her could most easily be kept at bay by the performance of ritual, in much the same way as the terminally ill attempt to shore up the present, lest the uncertain dusk of their lives be inundated by the certainty of their futures. Her anger settled within her like the slowly sinking silt at the bottom of a deep, still pool. The old shapes of her life were worthless now, nothing but patterns of existence that carried no conviction beyond the mere preservation of her faith. What did it all matter now, when that which was instilled within her when she was nothing but a parcel of nerve and membrane inside her mother's womb could so easily wipe away what had been imposed upon her from the moment she had entered the convent?

She heard Father O'Hanlon waking in the next room and gripped the rail at the edge of the range, as if in the hope that it would anchor her to the real world. She listened to him exclaiming, reading the late hour aloud, exaggerating his rising from the armchair. The rosary beads click-clacked when he spilled them into his jacket pocket. He shuffled into the big kitchen. Her hands were busy with a glass-cloth, her mind fumbling for some semblance of normality.

'I had better go,' he said, hunching his shoulders, his fingers pulling at the lapels of the shapeless black jacket.

'But I don't want you to,' she said suddenly, realising that she had employed the wrong words as soon as they had left her lips. Their intimacy hung in the air between them. 'The children are restless tonight,' she lied. 'Maybe you would look in on them with me — bless them goodnight.'

Her hands twisted the cloth, pulling the fabric one way then another. She looked down from him, at the floor, at her feet, away, across the room, anywhere but at him. But she knew that he was looking at her. She could feel, and could not bear, the touch of his eyes upon her face, her skin, at that moment. She felt like a child that had just cursed in front of its parent. She waited for him to speak.

But he did not speak. Instead he turned away, and for a moment she hoped that he might not have heard her. He stood still, looking at the Madonna and Child, his hand rattling the rosary beads in his pocket. The room was so still that she could hear his breathing; coarse, as if strained through sackcloth. The stillness made her uneasy and she tapped at the floorboards with the edge of her shoe. The solid tick-tock of the clock in the kitchen came and comforted her in her desolation.

'Sister Michael,' he said, suddenly, startling her.

'Yes, Father.'

'I will see you for Mass on Sunday, will I not?'

His tone was different now and her heart sank. She felt close to tears. He took the bicycle clips from his pocket and stooped to press them around his ankles. She noticed his scuffed shoes again and felt a stab of pity for him. He straightened to bid her farewell, and though she searched for some form of contact with his eyes she knew that he would avoid it now.

Sister Michael watched him wheel the bicycle to the gate. He swung a leg over the crossbar and took off down the road. She waved but he did not seem to notice, and she closed the door; shutting out the cold, shutting out the light, as if they were all he had brought with him.

She did not see him for Mass on the following Sunday. He sent a young be-spectacled priest, fresh from Maynooth, in his place. The young priest wore a crisp new suit and shiny black brogues. When he placed the host upon her tongue there was a smell of soap from his fingers.

A CARNIVAL OF LIGHT

I CAN HARDLY bring myself to tell you what I have found here. It is not that I returned expecting to find everything as it was when you and I left; no, it is just that nothing remains now of our lives here. Everything has disappeared, crushed.

What I remember most are those tentative first days in the city. Summer days when we pulled the mattress from the corner of the room and set it out so that we could make love in the heat of the sun; and afterwards watch the leaved shadows of the plane tree outside play across our skin.

I have tried to forget all this.

The city is governed now by The Sole Authority. The stamp of their presence is everywhere, but I have yet to see a solitary official, enforcer, or employee of the Authority. They are nameless, faceless. No one will speak to me of them, no one will say how they came to power. But I see something in the people's eyes, in their turning away when I ask, even in their walk, that speaks of condemnation. What I do not yet know is whether it is the Sole Authority they condemn, or themselves.

While the leaf-shadows made shapes across our skin we talked. You told me of your hopes and ideals and I countered with portraits of reality, practicality. We talked ourselves into blind alleys, corners, and once there we would look at each other and burst into laughter, pause, and laugh again.

It was in laughter that we found a way out; before we both turned and saw that the leaf-shadows were camouflage.

All of these people seem to be employed. There are no drifters or idlers, no beggars or hustlers, no prostitutes or pedlars. Everyone walks the streets with a sense of purpose. They pass each other with little more than a cautious exchange of glances. Maybe it is enough for them that their breath might mingle in their wake.

Everyone walks, alone. I have discovered that the subway system was deliberately flooded at the very beginning. There are no buses, although the bus stops have not yet been removed. I have yet to see a motor-car. Trucks and vans carrying construction or cleansing equipment pass along the streets from time to time at great speed.

You see, there is little scope for contact among these people. The notion of society has been erased from everyday life, and replaced with authority and subjection.

It was about that time that you decided to become a poet. You wanted to leave behind your research at the Genetic

Institute and search out the relationships between things in a more imaginative way. For two weeks you sat in the room, out of the sunlight, writing in a heavy ledger, composing stanzas, rhymes and couplets that no one has seen. Then you returned to the Institute. You would not talk for days afterwards, but I let you be, hoping that in trying each of these things you would find yourself, and me.

I, as an architect, had dreams of turning the city into a poem. I lived that dream, but the dream has not outlived me. I surrendered it years ago to the baser projects of stairwells, plant housings, and space planning. That poem is dead now, but from time to time I rehearse the memory of it.

I have tried to track people down with my eyes, employing what must be our sole surviving common identity: that we are all human. At first they would look, startled that I have dared to catch their eye, their pupils dilating, swallowing my face for an instant; then spitting it out and returning their stare to the pavements, as if searching for something they think they have lost there. They recoil as if I have touched them; but it is the idea of contact that touches a nerve inside them.

Inevitably something, somewhere, gives. *Someone.*

A young girl approached me as I walked in the rain along the river embankment. At first, she walked past me, her wet hair flattened against her skull, rivulets crossing her forehead. I listened to her footsteps fade as I watched leaves swirling in the swollen river's surface currents. The footsteps stopped all of a sudden and then began again, steadily getting louder. She must have been standing behind me for more than a minute before I became aware of her presence there. I turned around and found her, looking straight through me, water streaming from the hem of her raincoat, filling her shoes.

'Hello,' I ventured. Although I waited some minutes for her reply, nothing came. She has never spoken to me, and towards the end I began to question her capacity for speech.

Eventually she walked back the way she had come and I followed a few yards behind her. We walked through the incessant rain for maybe two miles, without seeing anything else move other than the turbulent river at our side. She took me to the point where a set of narrow steps led down to the water, and there, two steps above the watermark, lay a sodden telephone directory.

In the beginning the room was almost empty, furnished only with the mattress and a small stool. The walls were bare. There were floorboards beneath our feet.

I was the first to clutter the space we had left alone.

You were silent as you watched me unfurl the new rug and throw it across the floor. I looked into your face, waiting for your reaction, but you simply stepped out of your shoes and walked across the rug. You stood there, in the centre of the rug, in the centre of our room, the centre of my life, your arms folded in front of you, looking out at the branches of the plane tree jostling in the breeze. I waited for you to speak.

'The leaves are beginning to fall,' you said, taking a step towards the window. 'Look. They're dying off, one by one.'

The girl stood at the top of the steps while I retrieved the book. I could tell by the look on her face as I came back up the steps that the telephone system was no longer in use. Rainwater continued to stream from her clothes and I offered her my coat, but she turned away.

As we walked back the way we had come I struggled to keep the directory in one piece. Parts of it turned to pulp between my fingers and binding glue ran from its spine. I still do not know why I took it back with me. It contained only the details of the people in the city at the time we were here. I leafed through its disintegrating pages, feverishly seeking out the names of those I knew, scribbling their addresses into the back of this note book. The familiarity of their names comforted me that night and I fell asleep in the hope that I would be spending the following evening with old, almost forgotten, friends.

Some time in the night I awoke. The rain was coming down harder than at any time during the day. I went to the window and looked out. The girl was still there, standing against a lamp-post, staring back at me, her hands behind her head, squeezing water from her hair.

Pieces of furniture began to appear in our room as if from nowhere. Bookshelves, a cabinet, a tall mirror. I returned one day to find that you had put the mattress on a base. It was now too heavy to move anywhere else in the room and I left it where it was in the corner.

We plundered the museum shops for art posters: Matisse, Cezanne, Kandinsky. They coloured the walls. Once, as I lay upon the bed, reading, I happened to look up at the Kandinsky above my head and felt that I was like a simple, solitary leaf falling into its vortex of line and colour.

Maps are banned here, and the streets are nameless. The Sole Authority has re-configured the road junctions. Many of the streets are blocked by high walls and the entrances to the housing projects have been moved around. Nevertheless, I managed to find my way after a week or so. The obstructions and changes to the fabric of the city have only served to strengthen people's memory. The Sole Authority has attempted to shore it up, but memory still pours through like water.

I went from one address to another, the girl always a few paces behind me, looking for those whose names I had rediscovered in the telephone directory. People just stared back at me, panic-eyed, their hands gripping the edges of their front doors. I said names over and over again until they turned and closed the door in my face. Even then I could feel their presence in the space behind their doors, waiting for the sounds of my departure, curiosity twitching in the hallway around them.

Towards the end of that week I found Catherine Fallon's name on the buzzer at the entrance to her apartment block on what was once Cursitor Avenue. (You remember the cypress trees there? They are gone now.) I pressed the buzzer and looked around while I waited for a reply. I pressed another time and looked up hoping to find Catherine or someone else leaning from their fourth-floor window, gazing at my head.

The fourth floor was gone. The upper floors of the block had been removed and replaced with a helicopter landing-pad. I stared at it in amazement as I walked around the building. Curtains began to twitch in the ground-floor windows and I left soon afterwards.

As I made my way back to the city centre I noticed many more landing-pads on the roofs of buildings. They were only noticeable if one looked for the tell-tale canopy around the edge of the building. I asked the girl why there were so many, but, as usual, there was no answer. I lay awake that night, listening out for the chopping of blades, cutting through the night sky. There were none. Only the infrequent rumble of the transporter trucks came to me.

It was true. As the room filled with furniture, the plane tree began to lose its leaves. More and more light poured into the room. I would open the door to find filigrees of sunlight playing together on the walls, braiding the corners, knotting the very air itself.

We talked less from then on. It was as if the light had bleached our minds, burnt our tongues. Words died upon our lips, orphaned into the air.

Our love-making was carried out in complete silence. It became urgent, and sometimes violent; something to be finished with as soon as it began.

We were mining different seams by then, you and I; cutting into the face of honesty.

I put off the search for our old apartment as long as I could. Of course I had it all worked out in my head within a matter of hours, and there was no real search in the end.

The girl was waiting next to the door as I emerged. Overnight, she had changed her clothes for the first time, and her chestnut hair looked newly washed and brushed. I smiled at her in the hope that her change of clothes signalled a change of heart. It did not. Her face remained as blank as ever. I shrugged and moved off down the street. She followed.

I had to walk in a complete circle to reach the block of apartments we used to live in. It seems that the Sole Authority has concentrated its street-blocking in this area. The whole neighbourhood is cluttered with high walls and dead-ends. Even the girl seemed disorientated and never fell more than a couple of paces behind me. Once, when I stopped all of a sudden, she walked into my back. I felt the ache of her body heat against my skin for a moment before she recoiled from me. She was more wary after that and kept her eyes fixed on me as we walked.

Once I had turned on to the street I knew instantly where everything was around me. The force of recognition hit me like a silent, invisible fist; swinging through the air, through the years of my life.

I stood very still as if listening out for a heartbeat. I heard the girl's feet scuff to a halt. She drew back and I knew that she knew what this place and this time meant for me. Not a word had passed her lips and I had told her next to nothing, but there, behind me on the empty, echoing street, beneath the concrete-grey sky, she knew my inner-most thoughts. She knew why I had come back here. She knew what returning was.

What can I tell you about how I see the end of our time together? What can I tell you about those last few days, when the last of the leaves had fallen from the plane tree and turned to dust beneath our feet?

Nothing.

I don't even want to think about it now. As I said at the beginning of all this, what I remember most are those first days. I want them to remain in that leaf-dappled light; like an under-exposed photograph of how it was.

I didn't know what to expect. Maybe it would have been

better if the building had been pulled to the ground, or shelled-out and blackened by fire.

It was just as I remembered it: the rust-streaked walls, the false windows on the ground floor, the pair of wire flower baskets hanging empty from the portico, like bird-cages. In our time children played games in the swinging skeletal shadows of those baskets. The shadows still swing, but now there are no children in the city. Who would wish anyone born into this?

The door was locked and I dared not force it. I walked around the back of the building, through the small parking-lot, and found the fire escape. It took me a few tries before I managed to unbalance the counterweight and release the ladder. It slid down to my feet, as if inviting me to go up.

I looked around for the girl. She was sitting on a low wall at the rear of the parking-lot staring at my face. Her almond eyes followed me as I began my climb up the side of the block. Every now and again I stopped and looked back at her. She was expressionless, but there was something in the tilt of her face that led me to believe that she approved of my actions, almost as if she had some foreknowledge of what I would do.

I crept up the ladder, noticing that the sky was darkening considerably. Night was flooding in. At the second floor I stopped and crouched on the narrow structure for a few moments. I crouched as I had crouched there years ago, my ear pressed to the ventilation grille, listening to you weeping on the night that I had said that I was leaving. I had wanted to burst in through the window and grab you and tell you that I wasn't going to leave after all, but I held back.

It was then that I remembered the plane tree. I stood up and looked around the angle of the building, reminding myself that it was autumn, that its leaves should be copper by now.

The tree was gone. A paving-stone at odds with its neighbours marked the scar on the ground below me. I looked down at it for what felt like an age, but was probably no more than a minute.

I scrambled up the remaining flights of steps and hauled myself on to the flat roof. When I looked back down the girl had moved towards the bottom of the fire escape. I beckoned to her to join me but she remained there, as emotionless and expressionless as ever.

The skyline, that famous skyline, has hardly changed. On the surface, nothing has changed here. On the surface, nothing had changed between us.

The apartment blocks that rose higher than ours on either side have not changed, with the exception that the taller of the two now has a helicopter pad perched on top. I walked around the roof, the tar-paper crackling beneath my feet. I expect that it still leaks as I haven't seen any signs of recent repair.

I walked in a circle for a while, as if willing myself to walk back into history and see if I could find anything new there. Of course I understood that by returning here I was simply living in the past, but I was happy to immerse myself in it, to reach for it and clutch it to me, never letting go.

The gentlest of breezes tugged at my clothes and I looked out to where that breeze was travelling. The roof-tops seemed to return my gaze. Even the light in this city seems not to have changed in all these years. It is old light; dull, anxious, pent-up like so much else here; waiting.

Nothing decays here. Not light, not life. Not even memory.

I sat there watching that same, tired light darken. I listened out for birds and cicadas, radios and traffic. There was only silence, a dead noise, and the night wind fluttering the pages I wrote upon. The windows of the apartments overlooking the roof were dark. I imagined the occupants sitting or lying around inside, no sound but that of their own breathing. The television is tuned to a dead channel. It blinks in the corners of their rooms. They are all waiting.

They, too, are paralysed by memory.

Eventually my attention drifted towards the cabin that housed the elevator motor. Its door shuddered open, fragments of rotten wood flying from its edges. I pushed it open so that what light there was would allow me to see inside. The elevator no longer worked. The wires were wrapped around the pulleys, plagued with rust. The shaft had not been covered over but it is hardly dangerous since it appears that no one has been there since you and I left on that Halloween night. I felt along the shelves and spaces around the shaft, retrieving only handfuls of dust, paper and feathers. I don't know what I expected to find, but my fingers brushed off something plastic. Reaching across the angle of the shaft I pulled out a bag of sorts and threw it behind me on to the roof. It split open, sending its contents rolling in all directions. I staggered around the roof for a few seconds grabbing at the slim, light cylinders in the darkness.

Fireworks. I could hardly believe my eyes. I had found the fireworks you and I had left behind on the night that we left this city. There were maybe thirty of them: rockets, Roman candles, Catherine wheels, double repeaters, starbursts. I rolled them over and over in my hands, feeling for dampness. They appeared to be dry, intact.

I squatted down on the roof and looked at the fireworks again and again. I was shaking with excitement. The possibility of bringing colour to this dead city filled me with delight, with hope.

Never, in the years since we parted, have I felt so full of hope. Not the hope that things would be the same again, but that each of us would rediscover something neither of us knew we possessed. Even if it cannot bring us back (or closer) together, at least we will have drawn each other towards something valuable, something worthwhile. Rediscovery is everything for me now.

My imagination draws for me a picture of you standing at a window that overlooks a shallow-cupped bay in Mayo.

In the room behind you, two young children romp around a play-pen. A man's donkey-jacket hangs on the back of a door. I see your arms folded beneath your breasts, one hand gripping this notebook. Outside, yellow bursts of gorse bush tumble down towards the strand. Beyond the bay are countless islands (one for each day of the year, or so you once told me) standing in the water, waiting. You lift your gaze from these sentences and focus upon the islands, looking away from the world you live in, as if searching for a truth out there.

I don't know what you see.

It took me a while to set up the fireworks. I found a few blocks of wood in the elevator cabin and managed to wedge the rockets between them so that they pointed into the sky. Although I stopped smoking eighteen months ago, I have always carried around the lighter your parents bought for me.

Once the fireworks were ready to go I walked to the edge of the roof and looked around for the girl. She was sitting on the low wall that surrounded the parking-lot, almost invisible in the shadows.

'Climb up here,' I shouted, 'you'll like this!' Even as I spoke I knew she would not respond.

I filled another page of this notebook, and took the precaution of writing your address on the cover so that if I were to lose it, these words might find their way back to you. It seems inevitable that *I* will not.

The flame trembled when I went to light the first blue touch-paper. It took eventually and the sparks travelled into the base of the first rocket. I leaned back and watched as the rocket sprang from its mooring and sped into the sky. The noise was deafening, coruscating between the buildings on either side. I quickly lit two more touch-papers and moved back just as the first rocket burst over the city, showers of green starlets singing in the air. It was joined by two bursts of scarlet. The sky lit up as each firework exploded, and I caught their dazzle in my eyes. The cacophony of cracks and bangs tore through the silence that has enveloped this city. I lit the pair of Catherine wheels that I had fixed to the frame of the elevator cabin. They rotated slowly at first, but gathered speed until they became blurred discs of colour, throwing hot sparks in all directions.

As each firework erupted into life I watched and watched, feeling that some weight was lifting from me, as if the light itself poured out of me. And as I watched, lights came on in the apartments overlooking the roof, families crowded along the windowsills, straining their eyes and hearts into the night sky, watching the fireworks breaking against the darkness. A few of them shouted across at their neighbours and others clapped. It was as if by stealth that I had entered and re-opened their eyes.

The fireworks continued to burst above my head. They launched their fiery particles into the air like seeds bursting from a dry pod.

Then, in the fragment of silence between one rocket and another, I heard a distant thudding beating through the air. The people in the windows stopped clapping and shouting. I saw them turn their ears in another direction. Slowly, reluctantly, the windows closed, one by one. As I lit another pair of touch-papers the lights went out in all the windows. The Catherine wheels slowed to a halt.

I am standing now, in the shadow of the elevator cabin, at the edge of the roof. Fireworks are still going off above my head. By their light I can manage to scribble this last page to you. The helicopters are hovering nearby, their spot-lights trained on this building, the sound of their blades tearing through the air. One of them is attempting to dodge the fireworks and land on the neighbouring pad. Below me, the girl is jumping up and down, her arms outstretched, a smile across her face for the first time, the colours of the fireworks reflecting upon her skin. When I am finished I will drop this notebook to her.

This might be the last you will hear from me. And if it is, do not come here to look. I can only hope that if you look anywhere, your heart is where you'll find me.

MAGNETS

THIS MAY NOT be all that important, but, I am a drawer of maps. A cartographer. As a child I was always looking at maps. Maps pinned out upon the cold walls of my classrooms at school, or brittle, yellowing ones on the dashboard of my father's car that smelt of tobacco and rattled with dried out pine needles from the day we went to the Blue Forest. Ever since taking those first imaginary steps across pale ochre foot-hills, mid-green valleys, and aquamarine ocean trenches I had wanted to render the intricate details of landscape upon a page.

Now, some twenty or so years later, my craft is reproduced in atlases, gazetteers, and ordnance survey maps across the world. My steady lines and scaled representations have not by any means made me a rich man, but they have made of me a man satisfied by what he has achieved through his work. There are few things more wonderful to me than the detailed, ordered expanse of lines, colour and lettering spread out over what was a few weeks beforehand a dull, featureless membrane of paper.

Tonight I am sitting at my drawing-board set against one wall of our living-room. I have the light-box switched on under a map on my board. It pours light out through the paper and etches contour lines across my face and along the ceiling above, the lines disappearing into the shadows at the corners of the room. Apart from this the room is in darkness. Sometimes, when I feel low, I make the darkness even more complete by switching off the light-box and shutting my eyes, hoping that when I open them again my trouble will be gone. Gone, like a daydream that you suddenly lose hold of in your brain, as if it was never there in the first place.

My trouble is that my wife, Marsha, is dying. The doctors can only tell us that she is suffering from a nervous disease. Neurological. In their sparsely furnished consulting-rooms they hang blue and black X-rays in front of light-boxes and talk of motor neurons, potassium, and synapses. They draw haphazard diagrams in vivid red ink on overhead projector screens to illustrate to us why Marsha will die in a few weeks', months', or years' time. Together we sit there as if at the cinema, watching this instructive cartoon about the chemistry of her death. There is only so much they can tell us, they say, as there is only so much they know.

Before this illness Marsha was a painter. She would often take herself into Dublin to render its Georgian windows or the Gothic arches of Christchurch Cathedral in oils and acrylics. On the odd weekend I would help her hang her canvasses and boards on the green railings of Merrion Square, hoping to sell a few to passers-by. Now life is making careful plans to paint her off its canvas. Her patch of railings in Merrion Square will be as bare as a virgin canvas waiting for colour. A colour which will not come.

I hear her cough in the bedroom as she awakes briefly from her troubled sleep. Our baby son, Matthew, does not stir in his wooden cot at the foot of our bed. The plastic tubs of pills sit in a tidy stack on the bedside table next to a pitcher of water and solitary drinking-glass. The sterilising unit on the dresser hums from time to time as it reheats its vital contents: syringes, drip connections, an assortment of needles and valves. This mosaic of sound drifts out to me from the bedroom like whispers off a ghost-ship.

I turn off the light under my drawing-board and pull back the curtains on the bay window at the front of the room. I haul up the armchair and sit where I can see all the way across our small front garden and out on to the street. Outside it is snowing heavily, the flakes bumping silently against the window panes and collecting on the frames and sill. They have been collecting there for three weeks now. Our town has become like an old, rheumatoid man, stirring for a short while at midday to venture out and feed itself, then scurrying back into its small houses under thick blankets of white snow. A few slow cars roam the streets but their tracks are soon filled in. The schools shut two weeks ago, and the children have long since tired of snowballs and toboggans. The town is waiting for the snow to end, for the green and dirty-brown earth to show through, waiting to see the streets energised with sunlight.

I see my blue reflection in a single pane of glass, my eyes

set in looming hollows in my forehead, my chin melted into the shadows at my neck. The frail light is focussed on my nose and mouth, as if there was nothing else of me worth illuminating. Maybe there *is* nothing else. After all, we are barely here on these drifting, colliding continents. Little more than snowflakes blown and eventually crushed in the world's snowstorm. Brief flurries in time, waiting to melt into the past.

Something stirs in the bedroom behind me. I hear the bed creak and the floorboards flexing under her feet. A trickle of water from the glass pitcher on the bedside table, a moment of suspended silence, and then her unsteady shuffle across the carpet. I pretend not to hear anything and keep my face turned towards the window. Except that I am watching her dull reflection in the glass. I can scarcely make her out in the darkness, just about manage to see her shape flit through the doorway from the bedroom. She is wearing the dressing-gown she bought me on our first Christmas together – she has worn it ever since. It takes her maybe two minutes to shuffle up behind me. These minutes stretch out in the air between us until I feel they will snap. I watch her holding herself in taut concentration on each step, a climber on a rock face. I get a tightness behind the eyes and a warm flood around the vessels in my chest when I see her in moments like this.

Then she does something that takes me by surprise. She reaches her hands around my head and clamps her fingers over my eyes. I feel the warm fug of her breath on the nape of my neck and then her moist tongue touches me there. When it departs, the film of saliva grows cool in the air and puckers my skin. Still she has her fingers over my eyes.

'What's wrong?' she asks. 'Don't you want to go to sleep yet?'

'No, it's not that. I'm just thinking about things. I couldn't work for much longer anyway. My hand grew unsteady for a while.' I lift my right hand up into the range of my blind stare for her to see. 'It's okay now though.'

'Were you thinking about us?'

'And other things. Couldn't you sleep? Are you sore?'

'I was too warm, that's all. So I got up to cool off a bit.'

She removes her fingers slowly from over my eyes and then moves over into the space between me and the window. I rub my eyes and then look up at her standing there against the light from outside. She is barely there at all. The flesh has been secretly stripped from her bones by the stealthiest of thieves. She comes to sit across my lap and drapes one fragile arm around my neck, her fingers gripping my collar. I kiss her on the forehead and plant my hand in the hair at the back of her head.

When we last made love I was reminded of one time when I had held a bleating moth in my cupped hands. It bumped softly around my palms, dusting my skin with silver so that afterwards, when I opened my hands and let it soar upwards to the light-bulb, I would look at my palms and know that it had been there, had fought, had survived.

Marsha's skin flakes off in transparent showers, her hair drops in twos and threes, but she is still strangely beautiful.

'Don't you feel like doing something really special to-night?' she says, her voice muffled against the cloth of my shirt where she rests her head on my chest.

'Special? Like what?'

'Like going up to the hills again. Like we used to before ... before this.' She places her hand at the base of her slender throat when she says this. I clench her little finger in my fist and squeeze a little.

'But that was during the summer. We haven't been there in ages.'

'Not since Matthew was born,' she says, glancing over my shoulder towards the darkened doorway to the bed-room.

I look out through the window again at the street outside. The snow has eased considerably, and the clouds have cleared. Only the odd flake dies on the glass. The moonlight transforms everything. Shadows stretch out across the undulating layers of snow, picking out its crests and hollows. The snow out on the street looks so crisp and pure that for a moment I do not want to destroy its carefully constructed symmetry by driving the car across it.

'Okay,' I hear myself say. 'Let's do something special tonight, let's go back up to the hills and see what there is to see in the snow.' She grips me tighter than ever. I feel her dense warmth poking through my shirt like the lost rays of the sun. I scoop her up and stand for a second in front of the window, looking at our reflections in the glass. Her eyes are shut at this instant and her face seems to have settled into peacefulness. She is no weight in my arms.

Outside, the car is covered in snow. I scrape a couple of inches away from the windscreen and peel up a corner of the plastic sheeting underneath. It comes away slowly, making the snow wrinkle and creak before sliding in rigid, oblong shapes off the car.

Soon I have the engine running and the heater humming inside the car. Marsha sits on a stool just inside the front door watching me shovel snow from around the wheels. At her feet is a down-filled sleeping-bag. From time to time I pause and lean on the shovel to look back at her, my reddened face returning her smiles. A few snowflakes blow about in the slow draughts of wind. She stretches out a thin, upturned palm and some flakes come to rest and dissolve there against her skin. She goes away for a few minutes and by the time she returns with Matthew cradled against her chest I have the sleeping-bag tucked around the passenger seat, and a heavy blanket waiting for my son. Then I check the snow-chains and carry them both to the car.

The car scrapes and slides for purchase on the icy surface before I get used to it; first letting the car slide for a while in the direction of skids and then gently turning it back on to a straight line. We pass a stationary police-car, its revolving blue light bouncing off the snow and casting eerie shadows into the street.

'Do you think the snow is going to end soon?' she says, looking out through the side-window at the drifts banked on the roadside.

'I hope so, love. I hope so.' I reach to squeeze her behind the knee and she places her palm across the back of my hand and holds it there for a while. She looks up at me when I pull my hand away to take the car out of a long slide.

'Maybe when the weather improves we could go to the seaside again,' she says. 'How about Tramore, or even Youghal? Hmm?'

'Yeah, sure. If it gets warm enough I could take Matthew for his first swim, and we could write our names in the sand with razor shells . . .'

'And then let the sea wash our words away,' she sighs. She turns to look back out through the side-window. We are silent for a while after she says this, each thinking our own thoughts, mulling over her words.

The car struggles up the road away from the town and into the hills. Every so often the wheels spin in loose snow and we slide backwards a few inches. Each time this happens I can sense Marsha stiffening in her seat, and when the car begins to move forward again she lets out a shallow breath that condenses on the windscreen. Large clumps of snow drop from the overhanging trees on to the roof and bonnet as we pass underneath. They make soft booming noises on the metal, like distant thunderstorms.

'This is as far as I can really go,' I say, bringing the car to a halt on a ridge overlooking the town.

'This is fine,' she says. She leans across me and looks through the patch on the glass where I have cleared away the condensation with the edge of my hand. 'It's perfect.' She touches her lips to mine and brushes the cold tip of her nose along my cheekbone. I put an arm around her shoulder and hug her close to me. We sit like this for a minute or so, our eyes closed, listening out for the creaking snow and the slow, rhythmic breathing of our son in the seat behind us.

'Can we go outside?' she says. She has her fingers around the door latch. She pulls it to her until it clicks and the door springs a little out of its frame. Cold air seeps in through the gaps.

'Just for a minute. Then we had better be getting back in case it starts snowing again.'

Marsha pulls the sleeping-bag up around her and I hoist her into my arms and carry her out of the car. I sit her on the bonnet facing back towards the town and stand beside her, clutching her to me.

'Look at that,' she says, indicating with a nod the town on the plain below us. It appears like a discordant stain on the white expanse of snow, little seepages of light trailing out from its centre, then dying in the landscape. Lights come on and off from time to time. 'Blinking and sleeping,' says Marsha, 'blinking and sleeping.'

Specks of snow are beginning to catch in her hair. She pulls the sleeping-bag tighter around her and looks up at me. Her huge, dark eyes are turned upwards, watching the sky, the stars, the falling snow. She blinks and I feel a dense presence in the air between us, like magnets. Then I notice the tears stepping down her cheeks and suddenly hold her even closer to me, my breath destroying the snowflakes in her hair.

'Keep going, Sean,' she says, 'keep going. You know how these things cannot happen again. We're just here for now, for moments like these.' The words come out in her shallow gasps of breath.

'I know, love. I'm not so afraid any more. If only we could reshuffle the cards, but we can't. How frail we all are, how insignificant.'

My eyes sting with tears. She pulls herself up a little and touches her lips to my neck. I hold her there for a moment before putting an arm under her legs and carrying her back into the car. She watches me crossing in front of the headlamps and getting into the driver's seat. She places a hand over mine when I go to put the car into gear.

'Remember what I said, Sean. Don't forget.'

I twist my thumb up and around her finger and squeeze it while I look into her face. 'I won't forget, love,' I say. Then I slip the car into gear.

It takes a lot of tugging at the steering-wheel to turn the car around on the narrow road, but eventually I manage and we begin the journey home. The snow is falling heavily once again, blowing in clumps across the long, tubular beams of light poking out from the car into the night. The temperature is dropping.

I pull the car up outside our house and watch the headlamps fade quickly to orange on the snow before turning to Marsha to tell her we are home. She is sitting on her hands. Her head has slipped back against the head-rest and there is the faintest of smiles on her lips. Her unseeing eyes swallow the darkness beyond the glow of the dashboard-lights. I sniffle back escaping tears as her words float back to me. I squeeze her behind the knee. I don't know what to do next so I switch on the left indicator light and sit there watching the amber light flashing across the surface of the snow, like an alarm call in the middle of the night that nobody hears. Frost has formed in her long since condensed breath on the windscreen. It makes lines like the contours of a map: cliffs, valleys, a continental shelf. The ocean floor.